The Wedding Planners

Planning perfect weddings...
finding happy endings!

It's the biggest and most important day of a woman's life—and it has to be perfect.

At least that's what the Wedding Belles believe, and that's why they're Boston's top wedding-planner agency. But amidst the beautiful bouquets, divine dresses and rose-petal confetti, these six wedding planners long to be planning their own big day!

But first they have to find Mr. Right....

This month:
The Heir's Convenient Wife
by Myrna Mackenzie

Photographer: Regina's wedding album is perfect. Now she needs her husband to say I love you!

And don't miss the exciting wedding-planner tips and author reminiscences that accompany each book!

Myrna remembers her own wedding through the photos that mean so much to her:

"When I realized that I would be writing a story about a wedding photographer, I felt a special connection, not because I'm a photographer, but because wedding photographers record stories much as writers do.

Of course, I had to pull out my own wedding photos and live the story over again. There we were, my friends and I, getting ready for our walk down the aisle, pulling out cans of hair spray and fastening each other into our dresses. There's my husband with his brothers, clowning around for the photographer. There he is playing tennis that morning. It's a day that's frozen in time, caught on film forever, the beginning of a story. There we are, my husband and I, smiling as we begin our new adventure together.

Not everyone in those photos is still in my life, of course. Lives change, people move and sometimes we just forget to stay in touch. But during the course of writing this book, an old friend I hadn't seen in a long time, who had been my maid of honor (and I hers), called me out of the blue. It was coincidence, but it made me think about my wedding and the turns our lives had taken since that day (my husband and I happily continue the adventure, but I don't use hair spray anymore. He still plays tennis.).

Wedding photos do tell stories, and now and then it's good to look at them and remember how a fairy tale begins. *Once upon a time there was a man and a woman who met, not realizing they would get married, but did....*

Or...in the case of Regina and Dell, the hero and heroine of my story: Once upon a time there was a man and a woman who never thought they would stay married...."

For Myrna's latest news, visit www.myrnamackenzie.com.

And don't miss http://harlequin-theweddingplanners. blogspot.com for more wedding fun!

MYRNA MACKENZIE

The Heir's Convenient Wife

The Wedding Planners

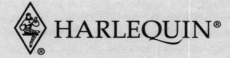

HARLEQUIN®

TORONTO • NEW YORK • LONDON
AMSTERDAM • PARIS • SYDNEY • HAMBURG
STOCKHOLM • ATHENS • TOKYO • MILAN • MADRID
PRAGUE • WARSAW • BUDAPEST • AUCKLAND

ISBN-13: 978-0-373-17513-0
ISBN-10:   0-373-17513-2

THE HEIR'S CONVENIENT WIFE

First North American Publication 2008.

www.eHarlequin.com

Printed in U.S.A.

Regina is the photographer at the Wedding Belles.
Here are her tips on how to get picture-perfect
memories from your big day:

❦ Shop around. Photographs are more than a simple record of an event. Different photographers have different styles, so visit several and examine their work to make sure that your wedding day images will be all you want them to be.

❦ Plan ahead. Photographs are the story of your wedding. Where do you want that story to begin? The shower? The rehearsal dinner? A wedding breakfast? Be clear and make your needs known.

❦ Your photographer will probably have ideas for places to take shots of the wedding party, but consider scouting out areas on your own. Think of places that have special significance to you and your groom, especially places you might want to return to on subsequent anniversaries for an annual photo to chronicle your special relationship.

❦ In this digital age, it's possible to choose only perfect photos, but consider the fact that some of the less-than-perfect moments may be the most precious. So don't discard a photo just because it's not a flawless moment. Look for the real and heartfelt shots, not just the pretty ones. This is the story of your day, and you'll want to cherish every tear and every smile.

❦ Take lots of photos, even more than you think you'll want. If you can't afford all professional shots, enlist friends. There is so much that you, as the bride, will miss, that you'll want tons of pictures to record those special times that may slip your notice. A wedding day is a one-time opportunity, so this is a case of more is better than less.

CHAPTER ONE

IT WAS a hot day in Boston when the curtain finally lifted from Regina Landers O'Ryan's eyes and she realized that she had made the biggest mistake of her life nearly a year ago. Now, because of her mistake, marrying the wrong man—or rather allowing him to marry her—her husband was paying the price. That had become clear this past week.

"Well, no more," she whispered to herself as she watched the clock hands move forward. Dell would be home soon. Normally she wasn't here when he arrived. She usually stayed in the darkroom developing photos for The Wedding Belles, the business where she and her friends worked making wedding dreams for other people come true.

The irony of the situation didn't escape Regina. Her business dealt in the kind of romantic dreams she no longer believed in. Still, *she* wasn't the one at issue.

Dell might still find the woman he would have chosen had he been given a choice. It was long past time to free her husband from his bonds.

Regina sat down to wait.

* * *

The minute Dell walked through the door of the tasteful mansion where he'd lived his whole life, he knew that something was different. And it wasn't the ghosts of old O'Ryan aristocrats that were raising the hair on the back of his neck.

Regina was perched in the hallway on a Victorian settee that had been in his family for generations and was just as uncomfortable as it looked. That in itself set off warning bells. Regina was never waiting for him when he got home. She rose to meet him now.

He looked into her concerned brown eyes. She was holding a sheath of papers.

"What's wrong?" he asked.

"We need to talk." Her soft voice came out unevenly. "We need to talk now," she repeated, clearing her throat and managing to sound firm and determined though she was clearly on edge.

"I see."

She shook her head. "No, you don't, but I do. Finally."

Regina held out her hand and he saw that the top sheet was a page torn out of a local magazine. "Have you seen this?" she asked.

He hadn't. The publication masqueraded as an event guide for the city of Boston, but the real draw was the bits of gossip sprinkled throughout its pages.

Dell lifted a brow. "Not my usual cup of tea."

She blushed slightly, and Dell realized that he'd rarely seen her blush. But then, he didn't really know Regina all that well. Their brief marriage had been entered into hastily for the sake of convenience, and they had spent very little time together. Like his parents had, they occupied this house as virtual strangers. But the delicate pink that tinted Regina's cheeks and dipped into the shadows at the vee of her pale yellow blouse definitely made him aware of her in ways he hadn't been when he'd entered the room. That was a surprise. It was also obviously bad timing.

Regina nodded, and for a moment Dell wondered if she had read his mind. "No, I suppose this wouldn't be the kind of thing a man like you might read," she said, "but I've verified the facts. They're true."

She turned away, her voice muffled, but she held her head high, her straight brown hair brushing her shoulders. Regina was a woman with generous curves, but she seemed thinner than he remembered her being when she'd fallen into his world just over a year ago. Was it any wonder? She'd been through a lot these past few months.

Dell rubbed a hand over his jaw. If Regina had suffered unhappiness, the blame was partly because of events that he had unintentionally set in motion. "You've verified the facts? So, tell me what they are, Regina." His voice came out too rough, and she turned to face him again.

"You were well on your way to marrying Elise Allenby when you—when we—"

"When we wed," he offered.

"Yes, but you did that to help me. You were supposed to marry Elise. Everyone was expecting an engagement announcement from the two of you. I didn't know. If I had, I wouldn't have—at least I *hope* I wouldn't have said yes." Distress filled her voice.

"Don't do that, Regina," he commanded. "You didn't destroy my love life if that's what you're thinking, and Elise and I hadn't even discussed marriage. I'm not a heartbroken man." But she was right in a way. Before the events of the past year had changed everything, he had wondered if he should deepen his relationship with

Elise. It had been a purely practical consideration. Dell had never been a romantic man. His life revolved around the O'Ryan empire, and Elise came from a highly respected family and was an intelligent and beautiful woman. She knew how to conduct herself at events and would have graced his table admirably when he had to entertain. He hadn't done any entertaining since his marriage to Regina.

But that had been his choice and not Regina's fault. He hadn't wanted to make demands given the circumstances. He hadn't felt he'd had the right to demand anything of her.

"Is she a heartbroken woman?" Regina asked, lifting her chin.

He blinked. "I don't know." What he didn't tell her was that Elise had come to his office the day after he'd married Regina in a private ceremony. It was the most emotional he had ever seen Elise. It was, in fact, the only time he'd seen Elise give vent to her emotions. But that had been almost a year ago. Still, it rankled that in trying to keep from hurting one woman he might have inadvertently hurt another.

Dell grimaced. "Why is this rag writing that kind of story now?" he demanded, taking a different tack. "It's old news."

"It's not old news to me. I don't want to think that I might have been the cause of another woman's pain."

"You weren't. It wasn't like that." Dell took a step toward her. "Elise might have thought we would eventually marry—others might have thought that as well—but I never suggested that to her. And if there had been reason…if I had made promises or if she'd been pregnant, I would have done what was right, Regina."

Regina sank back down on the hard mahogany of the settee, her breath *whooshing* out on an audible sigh. "I know you would have. You're…you believe in duty. You rescued me."

But it hadn't helped, Dell realized. Regina was no longer a woman in sudden desperate need, as she had been when they had wed. She had security and work that she enjoyed. But her eyes didn't light up the way they had when she'd shown up on his doorstep with some of his mail that had mistakenly been delivered to her house almost eighteen months ago. Unfortunate things had happened to her since that day, and he had been the un-witting author of some of those things.

"You know I haven't always done the right thing where you're concerned."

Regina's soft brown hair slid against the pale yellow of her blouse as she shook her head. "I haven't always done the right thing where you're concerned, either. Last week—" She frowned and began to pace.

Dell walked toward her, blocking her progress. He tilted his head, trying to see her expression, hidden as she refused to look at him. "What happened last week?" he asked.

Crossing her arms, Regina blew out a deep breath. "I was shooting a wedding when one of the guests, an older woman named Adele Tidings, noticed my name tag. She wanted to know if I was related to you, and once she knew that we were married, she wondered why she hadn't seen me around when she'd been at several func-tions lately which you had attended, alone. I realized how awful the truth would sound, and I didn't know what to say, so I just…lied. I told her that I'd been horribly ill for a long time."

"Regina, Adele is nice but nosy. She had no business asking you personal questions. Don't worry about it." But Regina shook her head.

"No, you and I both know that I wasn't sick. You helped me out when we wed, but I never even considered accompanying you to any of your social functions, even though I knew they were a part of your business. I didn't hold up my end of the bargain."

"We didn't make a bargain, Regina. We got married for good if unconventional reasons, and this year hasn't been your happiest. You have nothing to apologize for."

But the look in her eyes told him that she wasn't buying his argument.

"You never mentioned anything," she said, "but this article was written because there's a rumor that you've been approached to open a new store in Chicago. I assume it's true that one of your wealthiest customers is petitioning you to expand into her area and that she's started a campaign with her friends to entice you into moving. They're willing to wine you and dine you, to provide you with free advertising and do whatever it takes, but you've resisted even though it's a great opportunity. The city of Chicago would consider it a coup to get you, and the article says that people at the highest levels are wondering why you haven't at least looked into the matter."

Dell blew out a breath. "People often wonder about things that don't concern them."

"They're saying it's because your wife has a business in Boston and you don't want to upset her with a move."

She looked so deliciously miffed that Dell almost wanted to laugh.

"Maybe I should remind them that I have a business

headquartered in Boston and a fine old family home. Perhaps I simply don't want to expand to the Midwest."

She frowned, her nose wrinkling in that cute way it had. "Is that why?"

It wasn't. He loved Chicago and he had been thinking of expanding there for a while, but it would have been unconscionable to desert his new and fragile bride in her hour of need while he left town for the long periods of time that would be necessary to embark on such a venture. The gossips were right, at least partly right. No matter the circumstances, O'Ryans took care of their families and they took care of the family name. Leaving a wife alone so soon after they had wed would have stirred up more gossip than breaking it off with Elise had.

"I'm just pointing out that there's often more than one reason for doing or not doing something," he said, evading the question. "And I don't want you to worry about this. I'll handle it."

Regina stood suddenly and took a step toward him. "When I was ten and you were six, we didn't know each other, but like everyone else in the area, I knew who you were. One day I was walking past this house and your father was explaining to you why an O'Ryan couldn't run around barefoot in the summer the way the rest of us did. You had this longing look in your eyes and, not realizing that we lived in vastly different worlds, I felt sorry for you. I think I just saw a fleeting glimpse of that same look. The gossips are right. You'd like to pursue the Chicago connection, but you feel responsible for me. Well, no more. I don't want to continue our marriage, Dell."

Dell had been opening his mouth to dismiss her arguments, but that last sentence caught him by surprise.

As if someone had unexpectedly punched him square in the chest with a jab that was sharp and surprisingly painful. He blinked. "Excuse me?"

Then her words caught up to him. "Why?" he asked.

A sad smile lifted her lips. Her brown eyes looked equally sad as she held out her hands, then let them fall to her sides. "We married for the wrong reasons, ones that seemed important at the time. Partly it was because you wanted to protect me. And I—" She shook her head. "I was scared and lost and it was too easy to say yes, to want to be protected. I appreciate all you've done for me, all you've given up. You can't know how grateful I am. But I'm not lost anymore, and I'm not the type of woman who was made to be protected. Dell, we don't have a thing in common."

"We have a marriage in common." He didn't know why he was arguing. They *were* completely different kinds of people.

Regina laughed, a soft, pretty sound. "You know that's not enough. You're old money, good family, following the rules, doing what's required, what's right, while I'm a bit of a wild and fluffy mess and always have been."

He opened his mouth. She put up her palm to stop him.

"You don't need to defend me. I spent a lifetime trying to be what my parents expected and then finally realized that I was different. What's more, I'm good at being different, and I like the fact that I've finally accepted my creativity and my tendency to be unpredictable, but I don't fit into your world at all. I may be four years older than you, but you've always been the grown-up while I'll always be…I don't know. Me."

"There's nothing wrong with you."

"You're right. There isn't, but I'm not right for you, and—"

"I'm not right for you," he said, completing her sentence.

Dismay crept into her expression. "I didn't mean it that way. I'm not looking for romance. I don't even want it anymore, so you're not interfering with my love life."

"I'm just interfering with your life?"

"No!" Her voice was a bit too vehement, Dell couldn't help thinking, and he did smile then, even though he didn't feel at all like smiling.

"Liar. Being an O'Ryan probably isn't fun if you're not used to it."

She looked down at the magazine she still held. "People judge you, and I'm not helping your standing."

"Regina, I'm not worried." At least not about that. There had been good reasons why Regina hadn't appeared at his side this year. But theirs had not been an ordinary marriage. It certainly hadn't been what either of them would have chosen. And it hadn't been rewarding.

A pained look came into her eyes. "Every day women come into the shop. They're happy. They're marrying because it's what they want above all else, and that's as it should be, but it's not us. Admit it, Dell. This isn't working out. We're not a real couple. We don't even touch."

She muttered the last part, and Dell's senses began to sizzle. "We could touch," he told her, even though he had touched her only as a friend before their wedding night and never since. She had cried that night—long silent sobs she had tried to hold back. He had stopped. Since then he'd concentrated on just being a provider. He'd been willing to wait and be patient.

"No, we can't," Regina said softly. "It would be a lie. It wouldn't work."

He studied her. She'd obviously thought this through. "How do you know it wouldn't work?" he asked.

She blinked, clearly startled.

"The marriage, I mean," he continued. "Not the touching. How do you know the marriage wouldn't work?"

Regina's gaze met his. "It hasn't," she said softly, and he was pretty sure she was remembering the past months.

So was he, and what he was remembering was that Regina had been happy until she fell into his life and things had gone awry. He'd spent a lifetime learning to be a proper O'Ryan and protecting the O'Ryan reputation from any hint of scandal. But after he had married Regina and scandal had been averted, he had abdicated his responsibility as if his duty had been done. There had been no satisfaction in this marriage and yet...

"We haven't really tried to make our marriage work, have we?" he asked. "You mentioned that Adele wondered why she hadn't seen you around, but very few people have seen us together. Our marriage has been solely on paper, hasn't it?"

"There were reasons for that. You were practically forced to marry me."

Somehow Dell kept from reacting to that. "I *chose* to marry you, Regina." But he knew deep down that he was lying, at least partially. There had been numerous reasons why he had married Regina, but guilt, duty, honor and the need to protect the family name—and her—had been supreme.

But had he really protected her? Had he done anything right where she was concerned?

Maybe. After she had delivered his mail that day, they had become distant friends of a sort. She was nothing like the women he saw socially, nothing like the women he bedded and nothing like the women he considered as the ones who might produce the next O'Ryan heir. But he had liked her. She had been warm and refreshing. They hadn't known each other well, but they might have become friends if he hadn't made a single wrong and hasty decision that had turned the world upside down and had, ultimately, led to them becoming man and wife.

And now here they were, on the verge of another hasty, reckless decision. But he had never been a reckless man. Reckless actions were usually the result of messy emotions and he had spent years learning the ways emotional slips could ruin lives. Haste and recklessness fostered failure, and he didn't like failure.

"I *chose* to marry you," he said again. "But I've been a poor excuse for a husband, Regina. And I think that before we give up on this marriage, we should give ourselves a chance to turn this thing around."

Regina took a deep, audible breath. She paced a few steps, clearly agitated.

He followed her. When she turned suddenly, they were closer than they had been since their disastrous wedding night. Dell breathed in her light honeysuckle scent, and felt a small rush of attraction. Carefully he controlled his reaction.

"You don't love me," she said. "Elise—"

"No," he said. "I don't love you, but I don't love Elise, either. I'm not interested in love and would never have chosen that as a rationale for marrying. You just said that you didn't want love, either, so there are no impediments. I think we should begin again. Why shouldn't we stay married since we're already here?"

"Because now that I've had a chance to think rationally, I realize that I'm not O'Ryan material."

"Too late. You're already an O'Ryan."

"Only because of a few words in a ceremony I don't even remember."

"That counts."

She gave a cute little grimace, and Dell fought some primal male instinct to lean closer.

"Dell, this hasn't been a good year, but I'm—finally—regaining my sense of independence and balance. Help me out here. I'm trying to do the right thing."

He shook his head. "You're trying to do me a favor by setting me free to continue on my previous course, but divorce is the wrong thing if we haven't even tried to succeed. We're married, Regina, even if we didn't get here via the path your clients take. We should at least give ourselves a true trial run and get to know each other before we decide to divorce. There's a chance we might make a success of this situation, after all. We could save ourselves a lot of trouble and the kind of unpleasant publicity that comes to those in the spotlight who marry and then divorce too quickly. Does that make sense?"

She looked a bit unhappy but she nodded. "I guess so. Yes." Why did Dell feel that it was Regina doing him the favor now?

"How long a trial period?" she asked.

He considered. "How about two months? Long enough to get to know each other and become a couple."

"I don't know," she began. "This still seems unfair to you."

But Dell was warming to the idea. O'Ryans never did things impulsively. In fact, marrying Regina had been his only true impulse. His failure there was proof enough that slow and steady was best. For months she had been a silent stranger in his house, and he had accepted that. Now time was healing her, and there was renewed life in her eyes, vibrancy and spunk in her attitude and a woman emerging from the ashes. Yet he barely knew who she was. If they were going to end things, then he darn well wanted to know who he was divorcing. And if they were going to stay married, well…it was time to backtrack and uncover what had been covered. Methodically.

"If you're still worrying because we're not an ordinary couple, don't," he told her. "Not being in love is the best way. Love would only introduce complications and lead to possible rash mistakes. Emotional attachments would make it more difficult to end this later if that's where we finish up."

She had blanched when he had used the words rash mistakes and he cursed himself. She was probably thinking about her own past mistakes. He reached out and tucked a finger beneath her chin to distract her. "Let's give our marriage a fair chance," he urged.

Slowly she nodded, her soft skin sliding against his finger in a way that made him want to curve his palm against her jaw. "If that's what you want," she whispered.

He had no idea what he wanted, but he knew that when he decided, he wanted that decision to be based on logic.

Still, when he looked down at Regina rational thought slipped a bit. She had lifted her chin, and his finger had slid slightly down her throat, over silken skin that was made for a man's caress.

"How about the touching part?" she asked in a choked voice, as if she'd read his mind. His body tightened. But her deep brown eyes were genuinely concerned.

He cleared his throat. "We'll wait on that," he assured her, hoping his voice sounded normal. "At the moment we're just taking some time to make an effort and see if we're going to stay together."

"Or if we're going to part," she added, but he had the feeling that she had already decided that she wanted their marriage to end.

Maybe it would. They might be too different to make things work. But never let it be said that an O'Ryan walked away from a challenge or left a marriage before it was time.

Or left a bride unkissed. The phrase seemed to come out of nowhere. Just as Regina's newfound spirit had. Now that he acknowledged that he was attracted to this reborn Regina with the soft skin and berry lips, he was going to have to stay more in control of himself. This time they would do things right, by the book. Letting his impulses run away from him where his wife was concerned was not a good idea.

Especially since neither of them was certain if they would still be husband and wife by the end of the year.

But a vision of those full lips still lingered after she had gone.

CHAPTER TWO

REGINA was at her desk at The Wedding Belles late the next day pretending to review her week's schedule while she tried not to think about her future or the fact that it would soon be time to go home. The conversation with Dell yesterday had made her jumpy. Tall and dignified with that chestnut hair always in place and those unreadable amber eyes that seemed to measure everything, he was the picture of the elite male. Once again she had felt how ridiculous it was that a man like him should have been forced into marriage with a train wreck of a woman completely unsuited for him.

And that deep aristocratic voice of his always messed with her respiration and reasoning and made her feel as if she were babbling. She hated that. It reminded her too much of how her parents had always admonished her to be more normal and take the time for logic to kick in before she reacted to situations.

"If it were only that easy," she muttered. She wanted to be the type of sophisticated woman who knew how to talk sensibly to a man like Dell without feeling dizzy, but that didn't seem to be possible. Yesterday's meeting with him hadn't turned out at all the way she'd planned.

Suddenly she remembered that moment when he had suggested that they resume their role as man and wife and try touching each other…

Regina jerked at the thought and the pencil she was holding slipped out of her fingers. She lunged for it and knocked a photo album off the desk. It landed with a loud thud.

"Are you all right?" Julie's voice called from the reception area.

Not even close. Two days ago she would have honestly been able to say that she felt fine, but this new situation with Dell made her heart positively race.

"I'm great," Regina called, her voice muffled as she bent to pick up the album.

"Good. Could you come out here?" Julie's slightly tense voice had Regina hurrying past a cabinet filled with frame and matting samples and rushing into the reception area.

Late afternoon sunlight spilled through the tall windows, onto the golden-yellow walls and oak flooring, turning everything bright. It was closing time and most of the customers had gone, so the usual bustle of the shop was missing. Other than that, however, things looked pretty normal. Except for the dozens of containers of yellow daisies just inside the door.

"Where did those come from?" Serena asked, coming out of her own space, carrying a length of satin ribbon from the dress she had been working on. "Callie, did you order daisies for a wedding? I don't have any dresses on my list that would go well with that particular shade."

"Don't look at me. They're not mine," Callie said, her green eyes widening as she came out of the area where she created floral masterpieces and saw the mysterious display. "No orders for daisies lately."

"Nope. They're all for Belle." Natalie slipped some sample pictures of her cakes into her pocket as she bent down to look at the cards.

"You should have seen what it looked like when the delivery guy showed up with his arms full." Julie's reddish-brown curls bounced as she spoke. "I felt guilty sitting at the reception desk, it took him so many trips. Where should we put them?"

"I don't know, but Mr. Right must have been trying to create an impression." Audra gave a low whistle. "I've never heard Belle express a weakness for daisies, but as an accountant, I suppose I should admire the man's thrifty ways."

"So, the date went well, I take it," Regina offered. Belle had been introduced to the man through a mutual friend over the weekend and all of them had been hopeful that she might fall in love again.

"Maybe he *is* her Mr. Right," Callie said. The subject of whether there was a Mr. Right for every woman had come up lately at their weekly poker games. They'd all been friends for a long time, much longer than they'd worked together, and men were often a topic of conversation. And not always a comfortable one, Regina admitted. The friends were divided on their opinions, and some of them, herself included, had engaged in disastrous relationships. Was there a Mr. Right? It was possible. It was also possible that he might live on another planet and never show up, she conceded.

The click of a door sounded just then, and Belle came down from the apartment she kept upstairs, probably drawn by the chatter. The hard-to-ignore daisies and last night's big date in everyone's mind, the women couldn't help but look up. Not that that was unusual. Belle, an ample and gorgeous curvy woman with shining silver beautifully coiffed hair was a presence. She commanded attention without even trying. She was also the most generous, kind person Regina knew. She had inherited this building, she owned the shop and she cared for the Belles as if they were her daughters. They loved her, and it was only natural for them to wonder about the flowers.

"So…he's Mr. Right?" Audra asked, her blond hair sliding across her cheek as she tilted her head.

Belle gave a big sigh. "Hon, I'm afraid I've had my Mr. Right, and when my Matthew died that was it for me. I'm just looking for Mr. Maybe-We-Could-Keep-Each-Other-Company, but not with this man. He seemed nice at first, but then he got too grabby. He almost pulled a button off the sleeve of my best rose silk blouse."

"Well then, he's history," Regina said, giving her friend a hug. Belle loved nice things, especially clothes. "I take it he didn't ask first."

Belle returned the hug, her comforting scent surrounding Regina. "I almost had to damage him for other women," she said. "But I let him off easy by showing him the door and just giving him a quick wallop with my bag."

Julie chuckled. Belle's bag, a work of art, was huge.

"Looks like he's sorry." Natalie gestured toward the flowers. "Or maybe not. Those are some pathetic daisies."

"Sweetie, it doesn't matter." Belle's delicious Southern drawl stretched out the syllables. "That was the last straw. It wasn't even fun and it was downright embarrassing. Imagine a woman of my years having to wrestle with a man! Despite the fact that my friend Rae Anne keeps calling me to encourage me to hop back in the marriage market, I'm through dating, and I'm just going to sit back with those of you who are married or almost married and let the rest of the world look for love."

A chorus of objections echoed through the room. Regina and her friends might each have her own love or lost-love stories, but all of them wanted Belle to find a man who would appreciate her.

"I've got the shop, a good life and all of you girls for family," Belle insisted. "That's all I need. So, stop worrying about me. We've got weddings to plan and you have your own happily-ever-afters." She cast a maternal glance around, letting her gaze rest on each woman. When she came to Regina, Regina wanted to squirm. Everyone had been so worried about her this past year, and these were her best friends in the whole world. They cared about her. But revealing the details of her personal discussions with Dell would feel too much like betrayal of a man who had bent over backward to help her when she had desperately needed help.

"Dell might be opening a store in Chicago," she said instead. What was that surprised look on everyone's faces? "What?" she asked.

Audra shook her head. "Nothing. It's just that you tend not to volunteer information about your husband. Not without a lot of prodding."

"I know. I guess I'm just…" Not myself after the way that conversation went yesterday.

"I'm just excited," she finished, somewhat lamely. "Dell is very good at what he does, and it's—it's nice that his business is going so well."

Heavens, why was she babbling so much? Probably because she had just agreed to try to be something resembling a real wife to Dell, and she didn't have the vaguest idea how to go about that. Trying to transform herself into a genuine wife meant seeing him a lot more than she was used to, being near him all the time and considering the possibility that they might actually touch now and then.

The mere thought of that made her feel much warmer than the day merited. The memory of Dell's finger brushing her chin slid right into her mind. Where was a fan when a girl needed one?

"Regina, you're trembling," Natalie said.

"You must be really excited about Dell's new business venture," Callie added, one eyebrow raised.

"Yes, and Dell must be really excited, too," Serena said.

"What do you mean?" Regina asked, but her friend was staring out the window.

Startled, Regina looked out the window to see Dell, a stern, handsome figure in his black suit, headed toward the shop. Her heart began to trip in a ridiculous fashion.

"I—maybe he has some business with the shop," Regina offered, realizing how ridiculous that sounded. She knew why he was here. Their trial marriage was beginning in earnest.

"Hmm, powerful as he is, you don't exactly think of business when you look at the man," Belle offered.

Definitely not. Even wearing that serious expression, Dell was gorgeous, and several passing women stared at him as if they were about to melt right on the spot.

Regina frowned, even though she couldn't quite figure out why. "Well, yes, Dell is attractive."

Natalie raised an eyebrow. "You say that as if you've never noticed it before."

"Of course I've noticed." Even though that wasn't

strictly true. She had done her best not to notice, probably because their marriage hadn't seemed real.

"I don't think I've ever heard you say anything like that about Dell before," Audra said.

"Well, I should have. He's my husband and he does have a great body. I've thought it." The words came out so stilted and unnatural sounding that Regina half expected the ceiling to crash in on her.

For almost a year she had avoided even thinking of Dell as a husband. When they had wed, she'd been pregnant by his cousin who had deserted her, leaving Dell to save the day. He had, of course. After all, family honor and a baby's future had been at stake. Given the circumstances, it had been easy to think of Dell as a savior rather than a husband. Marriage had simply made them housemates, not more. And after her miscarriage—Regina struggled to breathe—she had ceased to think at all for a long time. But now…

"He's my husband," she said again. *At least for two more months.*

"Yes, we know that, sweetie," Belle said. "Apparently he does, too, since he's here."

Regina took a deep breath and looked down at her feet clad in eye-popping, chili-pepper-red espadrilles. Even after their talk about trying to have a real marriage, she had expected things to simply fall back into their former distant pattern. She would wait out the two months, living mostly in the shop where she felt free to be herself, and Dell would occupy his mansion and downtown office.

Obviously she'd miscalculated. Here he was in all his masculine glory, tall and powerful, the picture of a man of consequence. And here she was, slightly plump, less than willowy, a very ordinary woman who only exuded confidence behind a camera. They were so mismatched. This arrangement could have such dire consequences for her. But she *had* agreed to the plan.

"Regina? You're looking a bit dazed. Are you all right?" Julie asked, moving closer as if to protect her.

Regina nodded. "Oh, yes, I'm great. Just caught a bit off guard."

But there was no more time to prepare herself. Here he was, pushing through the door, causing the little bell to tinkle brightly as if to say, "Dell's here! Every woman in sight, start acting like an utter fool!"

Not me, not me, Regina told herself. She pasted on a smile, remembering their plan.

"Dell! How very nice to see you!" she said a bit too forcefully. Purposely she avoided looking in her friends' direction. She tried not to think about the fact that they would surely wonder why she had gone from a never-comment-on-your-husband woman to an idiotically smiling wife.

A look of mild amusement crossed Dell's face. "How very nice to see you, too," he agreed.

"I—is there something you needed?" she asked. "That is, I—what a surprise to have you show up here!"

Again, that look of barely concealed amusement flashed over his features. "We're married," he reminded her.

Regina looked up into his eyes even though she knew the danger of that. "I know." Actually she felt a bit like a newlywed today, a bride who barely knew her husband.

His gaze met hers, direct and unflinching and intense. "I thought we might go out to dinner together," he said.

His voice dipped low, and despite the fact that she knew that this was just Dell's way of making a concerted effort towards their trial marriage, Regina felt a little queasy at the thought of people watching her with Dell. What if she looked as besotted as every other woman and someone caught that look on film? How utterly embarrassing and humiliating would that be?

She tamped down her reservations and nodded. "Dinner together? That sounds…nice."

He laughed. "You needn't make it sound as if I'm forcing you to watch ten years of home movies."

Regina couldn't help it. She laughed, too. "Dinner *would* be nice," she agreed. It wasn't Dell's fault that he had such presence. "Let me get my purse and camera and we'll go."

As she passed her friends, they gave her questioning looks. Regina knew she'd been acting flustered, but to their credit they didn't appear to have interrogated Dell when she returned and were simply quietly chatting about Chicago. The Belles were protective of each other, but they also respected each other's boundaries. She loved that about them. They obviously realized she didn't want to discuss the details of her marriage.

Which was good, since there wasn't anything to discuss.

Until now.

Trying not to think about that, Regina headed for the door, calling goodbye. Dell slipped around her and held the door. He followed her outside into the fading sunshine, then handed her into a limo that seemed to appear by magic. But then, Dell had always been a man in control of every situation. Unlike herself.

"Thank you for taking me to dinner," she managed

to say. "I have to say, though, that it was unlike you to just show up." Dell was a man who always lived on a schedule.

He nodded. "Yes, but then we're in somewhat uncharted territory right now, aren't we?"

"What do you mean?"

"I've never been a real husband," he said in that deep, low voice that made her think about what real husbands did. *All* the things real husbands did. Like sleeping naked with their wives.

Okay, she was definitely going to have to stop those kinds of thoughts. "Well, I've never been a real wife."

"That's why we're going to talk. We left things rather open-ended last night. We need a plan."

Dell's deep voice rolled over her and Regina's palms began to tingle. She had never been good at plans. That was part of the reason she had done stupid things and Dell had been forced into marriage with her. Dell was very good at plans. He was the one who had proposed that they marry.

Unable to stop herself, Regina folded both palms across her heart, trying to calm herself down.

"Regina?" he asked, his voice filled with concern.

"We'll make a plan," she agreed.

"Good," he said with a smile that did awful, wonderful things to her insides. "I'm going to do my best to be the perfect husband."

Oh, no, don't do that, she wanted to say. This is a marriage of convenience. I don't even want to risk feeling more, a move that could be disastrous. But...

"I'll try to be a model wife, too," she said weakly. If only she could figure out how to do that while keeping this marriage risk-free. "Dell?"

"Yes?"

"What exactly *is* a model wife in the O'Ryan world?"

A look of dark amusement filled his eyes and he took her hand, running his thumb over the gold and diamond band that circled her ring finger. "Let's go to dinner," he said.

But he hadn't answered her question, had he? Maybe her answer wasn't important. He probably knew she wasn't capable of being a true O'Ryan. He had wed her out of pity and duty and honor and now he was stuck with her, a poor substitute for Elise Allenby who really would have been a model O'Ryan wife.

A slim and unfamiliar thread of pain ran through Regina followed immediately by a very familiar sense of indignation. She had spent her life trying to please and falling short, and had promised herself never to go that route again. Yet she hadn't said no to this marriage or this plan.

Well, Dell was the one who had opted to extend their wedding. He knew what he had for a wife.

Or did he?

Maybe I can be the perfect O'Ryan bride, Regina thought. But she didn't pursue that thought any further. Some things couldn't bear up under too much scrutiny, could they?

Sometimes a woman just had to fly on faith and hope for a miracle.

CHAPTER THREE

DELL watched Regina pick at her food. Had he been bullying her? Probably. He'd spent a lifetime learning to be an O'Ryan and sometimes it was difficult to remember that he didn't have to be that way with his wife.

His wife. How had that happened?

"Regina, before we begin, I want to say that I'm sorry for everything that's happened."

She stopped toying with her food and looked up, those deep caramel eyes studying him carefully. Regina had the most amazing eyes, clear and utterly transparent. He had startled her and now she was nervous. "I shouldn't have thrown you together with Lee," he clarified, then realized that it was the first time his cousin's name had been mentioned in a long time.

She shook her head. "What happened wasn't your fault."

"And if I insist it was?"

"You don't get to say." Regina speared a piece of asparagus. "What happened with Lee is on my head."

But she was wrong. That day when Regina had shown up with his mail had happened at a time when he was worrying about Lee, because Lee, orphaned young and raised with Dell, had been like a brother, a wild and socially awkward brother who had not been a hit with women. Regina's unexpected appearance and cheerful disposition had seemed like a gift, a woman who could give Lee the confidence he needed to take his place in the O'Ryan empire. So Dell had sacrificed her to his cousin, and everything that had happened afterward was on his conscience.

He opened his mouth to tell her so.

Instantly she leaned closer. "Don't do that O'Ryan thing," she told him.

Dell blinked. "Excuse me?"

Regina placed her palms on the burgundy tablecloth. "Dell, I know how much responsibility you have. The O'Ryan Gemstone Gallery is only one arm of O'Ryan Enterprises and it must take an amazing amount of work to manage something like that. You don't have to take responsibility for my problems, too. What happened to me this year wasn't your doing."

He drew his brows together, preparing to object.

"I need to get past it myself," she continued, not allowing him to cut in.

"All right, we'll drop that subject." Dell blew out a breath and sat back in his chair. Not that he was agreeing with her, but if she needed to claim responsibility, he would allow her to do that. This time.

Silence set in. Regina looked around her, surveying the elegant surroundings, the tapestries on the walls, the string quartet playing softly, the tuxedoed waiters. She fidgeted with her spoon and squirmed on her chair. "This is nice," she said.

Dell noted that she still hadn't eaten much. He smiled. "Not your style?"

"It doesn't have to be my style. It's your style. I don't really have a style, so at least one of us should have one," she said.

Dell couldn't help chuckling at that.

Regina smiled. He realized then that he hadn't seen a genuine smile on her face since their whole fiasco of a marriage had begun. And it had been her sunny disposition that had first told him she would be right for Lee.

Dell brushed that thought aside, but his gaze drifted to her lips nonetheless. She had pretty lips, plump but not overly so. The kind of lips a man would like to feel beneath his own. He could see why Lee had let things get out of hand.

But his staring was making her uncomfortable. A trace of delicious pink climbed up her throat.

"You should smile more," he said, almost without thought.

She gave an almost imperceptible nod. "I'll try to remember that. Smiling at each other should be part of our plan, shouldn't it?"

Oh, yes, the plan.

"I suppose we'd better start brainstorming," he agreed, glad that she had been thinking straight while he had been ogling her mouth. He reached into his jacket pocket and pulled out a small black notebook and a pen.

Her eyes widened.

"What?" he said.

"You're really very good at what you do, aren't you?" she asked. "I mean, of course, you are. You run an empire, you hire and fire people, you date fabulous women and command the attention of important people. Politicians and lawyers and media types and such."

"All that because I took out a pen and paper?"

"No. It was more the way you did it. You're going to make a plan and we're going to carry it out and you have no doubt that everything will go according to that plan. It comes naturally. You're an O'Ryan, and controlling the universe is in your genes." She said that as if it were a new discovery she had just made after having been married to him for many months.

"You seem concerned. Am I pushing you?"

She studied him for a minute, then slowly shook her head. "No, it's more a matter of you being so sure that things will turn out a certain way and me being nervous that I'll mess it up. I tend to just let loose and do things and sometimes that doesn't work so well. Although—" she lifted one shoulder in a shrug "—I'm not sure even I could mess up your game plan once you've set the course."

Ouch. He had worked hard at learning to be organized and in charge. Barreling through with a logical plan had helped his parents' disaster of a marriage survive, it had enabled him to overcome an early heartbreak and had kept him ahead of his competition in business, but he supposed that to someone like Regina he might appear overbearing.

"You're frowning. I'm sorry. I shouldn't have said…whatever I said." Regina's voice was soft.

He held up one hand. "You should say what you think. That's part of being married."

"How do you know?"

He smiled and shrugged. "I'm guessing."

She returned his smile. "Well, you probably *are* right about us needing a blueprint. And…everything."

He raised a brow.

"Okay, almost everything. I'm sure you're not perfect."

Dell's smile grew.

"Well, you must have *some* flaws," she reasoned. "Doesn't everyone?"

She looked so deliciously flustered at her frank words that he couldn't help chuckling.

"*You* are amazing," he said.

Pale pink tinged her cheeks again. Why had he never noticed that she was a blusher before yesterday? There was something wickedly delicious and erotic about a woman who blushed. "Amazing? Maybe your judgment isn't as good as I thought," she said, still visibly flustered. "Take your pen. Let's get to work. How do we go about trying to get started on our marriage plans? What should we do?"

Kiss was the first thought that came into his mind, but he quickly squelched it. This had been a difficult year for Regina, including an unexpected pregnancy, the betrayal of a man she had trusted, a hasty wedding and a devastating miscarriage. The two of them had started married life in a rush. He knew the mailman and the valet at the parking garage better than he knew her. When they finally touched, if they ever touched, he wanted her to know who she was kissing. Trust had to be established, and given her past, that would be impossible if he pushed her too fast. They needed time and more.

"I'd like to visit you at work again," he said, scribbling that down.

She looked startled. "Why?"

Because she had friends there who cared about her and would protect her even if he did something foolish. "I've never seen you at work," he said, and that was the truth as well.

"I've never seen you at work, either."

Dell thought of his office. Sophisticated, expensive,

oppressively dull. He loved his work, but the offices were the same as they had been in his father's time and his grandfather's before that. They reeked of the O'Ryan legacy and would be considered stuffy by modern standards. Regina was the epitome of modern with her cute little shockingly gaudy shoes, her digital cameras and her creative spirit.

"You might find it boring," he said, surprised that it mattered to him what she thought. He'd never cared for people's opinions before.

She crossed her arms, obviously trying to look firm. Instead she looked like an adorable kitten trying to wield control. "Fair is fair," she said. "If you visit the Belles, I should visit O'Ryan Enterprises."

"You're right," he conceded.

"What else should we do? I suspect that being a normal, married couple in my world and yours is a bit different. What do normal, married people do in your world?"

They sleep together, he thought. *They make love.* The thought brought instant heat to his body, and he forced himself to push it aside. "I think we should make our own rules. We've both agreed that we don't have a conventional marriage and what we're each looking for is…a partner?" he said.

She nodded. "A companion?"

"Of sorts."

"And you would expect…what?" She looked a bit nervous. His heart ached. Dell was willing to wager that when she had delivered his mail that day she would have never guessed that she would end up here today, in this way, with him, a man she would not have chosen to spend her life with.

"Relax, Regina," he said, reaching over and covering

her hand with his own. "I won't make you meet the queen."

Her eyes widened momentarily and then she laughed. "Good. I won't ask you to come with me to the seamier places I sometimes travel to when taking photos."

Dell let that sink in. Interesting and alarming. Had has wife been spending time in dark alleys and he didn't know about it? Was she safe? And could they bridge their gaps and make this marriage work?

He hoped so. It had been difficult enough dodging bad publicity when they had gotten married. Divorcing so soon afterward would only make the gossips and the media gather. They would dig deeper. The O'Ryan name would be smudged and Regina would be gossiped about. Her experience with Lee would no doubt be discovered and made public. Some might accuse her of being a gold digger, and that kind of thing couldn't help The Wedding Belles, the business that was Regina's life. So, if they could avoid divorce they should.

"All right," he said, just as if she hadn't mentioned the words seamier places. "Now that we've set a course, I'll want to meet the people you spend your time with." *And I'll want to make sure you're safe,* he thought.

"Dell, the shop isn't exactly a male kind of place. Are you sure?"

He smiled. "I'll be brave, and I'll stay out of your way. Let's just call this a beginning. Now about those seamy places…"

Frowning, Regina looked up at him. "I don't go there to embarrass you."

"I didn't say that."

"And I don't end up there often, but…"

He waited.

"In my spare time, I freelance, and I'm doing a pictorial on Boston. I cover a lot of territory and a variety of settings. Businesses, bridges, landmarks, artists, executives, homemakers, museum curators, hot dog vendors, homeless people and yes, sometimes prostitutes or addicts. I interview them. I listen to their stories. They let me take their pictures. It's my work," she explained solemnly. "It matters to me."

"Understood," he said. "But it's your safety I'm concerned about. I can hire people."

She considered that. "I don't think I'd feel comfortable with that, but I'll be careful. I always am, and since night photography isn't my specialty, I'm out in daylight, usually on Sundays. The risk is slight."

Their gazes met, held. Dell couldn't help thinking that their ideas of what constituted a risk might be different…

But she was already uncomfortable now, practically squirming from all his questions. He would file the subject away for later.

For now, he made a few more suggestions about things they could do and gatherings they might attend together. He'd make sure there was good publicity surrounding these events. Then, if things fell apart and she still wanted out once these two months were up, at least the world would know her as a real and valuable person, not just as the whirlwind wife of Dell O'Ryan.

"Dell?" Regina suddenly said.

He looked at her. She was clenching her water glass.

"I'm sorry. Have I overdone things? Is there anything we should change or omit?" he asked.

She sat up taller and took a visible breath. "I just want you to know that I'm going to do my best and give this a solid effort, no-holds-barred. In the end…we'll at least be friends, won't we?"

Their eyes met. "I hope we will if it comes to that." Maybe it would. No doubt this marriage had been far less than the salvation he had planned. She had obviously once wanted something with Lee that she had lost, and marriage with Dell O'Ryan hadn't been it. "You're sure you're all right with this plan?" he prodded gently again.

Regina looked slightly shaken but she nodded, her silky hair sliding against her shoulders. "Absolutely."

"All right then. We're on," he agreed.

"What do we do now?" Regina asked, looking around the rapidly emptying restaurant.

"We go home," Dell said simply, but as he stood to pull out her chair he realized that there was nothing simple about it. Beginning tonight they were moving down a new path, one that would lead them into the spotlight they had avoided thus far. As a prominent Bostonian he was used to having private moments showing up in the newspapers. Now that he and Regina would be spending time together, they would be on display. It wasn't the first time. When they had first gotten married, there had been photographers hovering, but after the two of them had failed to make public appearances together, the interest in them had tapered off. It would resurface, and there would be questions about why they were a couple again. The fact that Regina had suffered a miscarriage might come up.

Dell tried to block the automatic ache that assaulted him at that memory, but it was difficult. He concentrated on the fact that he would do what was necessary to protect Regina and to distract reporters from that topic.

That meant giving them something else to concentrate on. And now was the time to begin setting the stage with the media should there be any gossip miners around.

"I should—" *Put my arm around you,* he thought, but given their circumstances and the newness of all this, that seemed intrusive. Instead he reached down, his fingertips sliding against her palm as he folded his hand around hers.

She was warm, smooth, soft. His skin tingled. All he was doing was holding her hand, yet it felt like an intimate caress.

Regina looked down to where their hands were linked. "Of course," she said. "A married couple would do this. We'll go home." Where they would not be on display.

Where they could be private, Dell thought, then immediately pushed the vision of Regina in his arms away. She had just asked him for a divorce yesterday. She had agreed to a plan to get to know each other and nothing more. This marriage wasn't real yet, not in the true sense of the word.

And it might never be.

For the first time in a long while, Regina dreaded seeing her friends. The Belles loved her and knew her so well that they were practically mind readers. And the truth was that when she and Dell had arrived home last night, she had been painfully aware of him as a man in a way she hadn't been before.

That was risky. She'd been hurt by men who wanted to be friends but not more. And then there had been Lee who had left her pregnant and—given the fact that she'd funneled most of her money into The Wedding Belles business—with almost zero funds to raise a child. The whole scenario had been utterly demeaning and frightening.

"Now, I'm…"

Better, she wanted to say, but the truth was that she was a mess, she admitted, struggling into her jeans and slipping on a pair of electric-blue clogs with silver lightning bolts on the sides. This business with Dell was making her feel weird and uncomfortable. Even physically they were night and day, him being the tall, gorgeous, lean one and her being the ten extra pounds one. Moreover, she was socially not of his class, and their basic life philosophies would appear in two different volumes if there were encyclopedias that tracked such things.

The fact that they were now trying to think of each other as an actual husband and wife was making her crazy. He had held her hand, and her body had tightened in response. They had entered the house together, and all she could think of was what he must have done with other women in bed.

And then she had realized that he had probably been forced to give up sleeping with other women this past year and she hadn't been sleeping with him, either. It had been impossible not to wonder if he was feeling sexually frustrated or if she even made him think of desire.

"Agh!" she yelped, pulling on a powder-blue bell-sleeved blouse. "Don't even think such things."

Instead she should think about today and plan ahead the way Dell would.

"Okay, then," she said to herself. "When Dell shows up at the shop, the Belles are going to notice a change in the way we're interacting."

That was bad. She had been distraught for so long,

especially after she'd lost her child. Now that she was coming back to life her friends might think that she would do something foolish, like fall in love with another man who really didn't want her in the ways that counted. So if Dell brushed against her or took her hand and she trembled, they would definitely notice. That was how well they knew her.

Regina groaned. Her plan crumbled. She had agreed to give them a try, but she didn't think this new, shaky marriage could hold up under too much scrutiny, especially not the scrutiny of the people who loved and knew her best. Dell had saved her when she'd needed saving. He wanted a real marriage. She couldn't betray him by telling her friends the truth but she couldn't lie to her friends, either.

What if they asked him what was going on?

He's an honorable man. He'll tell the truth, she thought. He might even mention how practical they were being by pursuing a marriage devoid of love.

Then her friends would hate him. And if her friends hated Dell…

"Things will be beyond uncomfortable," she muttered. "Even a good marriage would suffer under those circumstances."

There was only one option. Keep Dell and her friends apart as much as possible until the marriage was either seriously settled or dissolved. But for today…

CHAPTER FOUR

"JUST so you know, Dell's stopping by today," Regina told her friends fifteen minutes before the shop was due to open.

Her friends all turned to look at her. "Wow, twice in two days after never having been here before. Anything you want to tell us about?" Julie asked.

Regina struggled for words.

"I mean, besides butt out of my marriage?" Callie asked.

That brought a round of laughter and helped Regina relax a little. "I know you're just curious because you care about me, but he's a good man," she said simply.

"All right, I understand," Audra said, which was saying a lot. After having been left at the altar, Audra had issues. "I do know there are some worthy males out there. Look at Julie's Matt or Callie's Jared or Serena's Mr. Perfect."

Julie smiled. The love she and her fiancé shared made her glow. Serena didn't glance up from the adjustments she was making to the dress on the mannequin, but lately Serena had been rather quiet about her own blossoming love life. Regina could identify. Some things were meant to be hugged to yourself.

But Callie openly grinned. She was well on the way to marrying Mr. Perfect and it was no secret. "All right, sweetie. You can't blame us for being curious about Dell's suddenly sociable ways, but it's your marriage. We'll back off. And actually, just having him here is a bit of a coup. He might be a draw to business and might create even more of a sensation than the Vandivers." The Vandivers were the Belles' big chance, a celebrity wedding, the biggest they had ever planned.

"At least he won't be as difficult as the Vandivers," Julie said. "Dell's always polite. Not like Liz Vandiver. What a temperamental bride."

"Yes, she's changed her mind four times about what kind of cake she wants," Natalie said.

"Five times on the flowers," Callie offered.

"But at least we've got the account," Serena added, and everyone agreed. The Vandivers were spending a lot of money and the very fact that the Belles had scored them as clients was attracting more business.

"Enough about the Vandivers," Regina said. "Their wedding may involve the most money but it's not the only one in town."

"Well, that's a relief, because we'd be out of business if they were," Julie remarked, earning a laugh. "But the Vandiver affair *will* be the most special one we'll arrange this year."

The rest of the Belles exchanged looks. "It's going to be impressive," Regina agreed, but Julie was going to have the most special wedding of the year. She just didn't know it yet. She and Matt couldn't afford all the trimmings for a wedding, so the rest of the Belles had decided to surprise her and give her a fairy tale send-off.

Regina tried not to remember how rushed and emotionless her own brief civil ceremony had been. At least her friends would have fairy-tale weddings. Callie, Julie and soon, hopefully, Serena.

Regina would never live the fairy tale. She didn't want to anymore. In fact, what she wanted…well, she didn't really know what she wanted. It wasn't her husband. It couldn't be her husband. Falling for a man like Dell when their marriage was only one of convenience would surely go down as the most foolish thing she could possibly do.

Still…he would be here any minute. Why was she so nervous when she hadn't been nervous around him mere days ago?

Probably because then Dell had only been part of the backdrop of her life. Now, she couldn't help thinking of him on more intimate terms and she had promised to show him her studio, a room that was very small and cozy.

Regina nearly groaned, but that would have attracted attention. Instead she went to her studio to try to create some more space.

"All right, tell me what's wrong, Regina."

Regina paused in her explanation of the difference between photographing wedding parties and other subjects and glanced up into Dell's eyes. Bad mistake. He had moved closer while she wasn't looking. She had to tip her head up. His lips would be within reach if she rose on her toes just slightly. The very thought made her feel warm and vulnerable.

"Why do you say that?" she asked.

He smiled. "Other than the fact that you're engaging in what I can only politely describe as speed-talking and the fact that you keep looking at me as if I intended to pounce on you?"

She grimaced. "Was I really doing that?"

"Am I making you uncomfortable? Should I leave?"

"No. No, it's not you. It's just…"

He waited.

"It's just, well I *do* feel self-conscious. This can't really be interesting to you."

Dell's amber eyes narrowed. "I thought we agreed to get to know more about each other. Your work is a big part of your life, isn't it?"

Regina looked around the room that had been her salvation many times in the past year. "I pour myself into it," she admitted. "Sometimes I probably get carried away."

"Then if I'm going to know you, I need to know… this." He held out one hand.

She understood. He had a list and a method. Making their marriage work was a business of sorts. Somehow that made her feel more comfortable, even though she knew it would distress her friends.

Just business, she thought. It's a simple plan. We get to know each other, we start to be seen together. We become a couple and make this marriage work. It made sense.

And yet when she looked up into his eyes to smile her agreement, she realized again just how close she was standing to him. His height, the breadth of his shoulders…her body felt too aware and sensitive.

She spun away. "All right, well, here we have some backdrops and I keep a few props for the brides. Sometimes I borrow things from the other Belles. Flowers or maybe a veil. Lighting is always important, and obviously the cameras and the computer are key. I still do some old-fashioned shots and use a darkroom but most of my work is digital these days. It's just more versatile and I don't have to worry about losing any shots, something that's very important for a wedding. Brides get very upset when there are gaps, but with digital cameras I can take pictures of everything, more than will ever be needed. I can take risky shots and cover the entire day. Sometimes I'm asked to be there for every aspect of the wedding, including the fittings, the bachelorette party, the shower, the rehearsal—"

"You didn't have any of that, did you? None of the things a bride should expect."

His voice broke in and cut her off. Regina glanced up from the piece of pink tulle she had draped across a backdrop and was fidgeting with. Dell looked concerned. He was studying her too closely. "That's what you wanted with Lee," he said quietly, "and it's what you should have had."

Okay, yes, she should have, but she was happy to be done with wanting the unattainable, and besides, Dell wasn't responsible. He might have introduced her to his cousin, but he was not the man who had deserted her. He was the man who had stayed, despite having no affection for her at all. He was also the man with a sense of duty so strong that he was here now making an effort.

She could do no less in return. So, ignoring the fears and warnings coursing through her, she smiled. "I got a lot more than I ever expected, Dell. I mean, have you seen your house?" she said, trying for a light tone. "It's absolutely gorgeous. I certainly never expected to live in a mansion like that."

He smiled a bit, but she could tell that he wasn't convinced or playing along. And her reference to the difference in their stations had obviously sent his thoughts elsewhere.

"I never even asked if I could help you with your

business," he mused. "I have plenty of money. You should have the best equipment, the newest cameras." He looked toward the area where she kept her cameras.

Any shyness or discomfort fled. Regina walked up to her husband. She tilted her head and gave him a stern smile. "No insulting my cameras. This ancient Nikon is war weary, but it was my first love. This Canon is beat up from use, but it signaled my first sale. They're special. They're almost like people to me."

He raised one wicked brow, and Regina melted. She remembered why women fell all over him. "People?" he asked.

"Good friends," she said, remaining firm. "Sacred stuff."

"Interesting." He stared at her, and Regina felt a low hum begin to run through her. The small room felt cramped. Dell seemed to fill the space. She had a terrible urge to step closer to him. This had to stop. Now.

"But if you really want to know what being a photographer is about," she rushed on, her words tripping out breathlessly. "I'll have to take you out in the field." Where there's open space and room to breathe, where she could not think about the power of the man she was married to.

"Out in the field?"

"You don't have to go," she said, wondering if she sounded hopeful. A woman could only take so much proximity to this man in one day.

"I don't want to make you change your plans."

But he already had. Her original plan had been to end their relationship and go back to her poor but comfortable existence where there were no devastating men making her feel flustered. Still, the kind of marriage

Dell wanted could be a kind of protection. Once she got past the achingly obvious virility of the man and got used to it, they could, hopefully, become friends.

A new friend might be nice. A male friend, that was. Love would never be an issue or a threat in her life again. Being married to Dell would protect her from all that. And, in that moment, Regina finally fell into the plan. She and Dell *could* make this work. They could really have a marriage without love but with companionship. That could be a very good thing, couldn't it?

She grinned at her husband. "I know how you love plans, but they don't always work. Today, for instance. No matter what you say, this can't be interesting to you. I can putter around here all day, but that's because I'm not seeing a vase of roses or a brass bowl." She motioned to two props on a table.

"What are you seeing?" He looked at the roses and the bowl and seemed genuinely interested.

She tilted her head. "I'm seeing a young bride throwing the petals in the air so that they flutter around her, brush her eyelids and rain on her shoulders as she smiles up at the man she's going to marry. I see a woman holding up the brass bowl like a genie's lantern, her heart full of wishes."

"I see."

His words seemed a bit cool, and Regina glanced at him, startled out of her reverie. "What?"

"Those are a girl's romantic dreams. The kind you gave up."

She felt her face growing warm and felt embarrassed. "No, they're not," she said, staring directly into his eyes. "They're stories, the kind a photographer weaves with her subjects. I happen to write love stories. That doesn't mean I'm interested in a love story of my own any more than a mystery writer is looking for the opportunity to go out and commit crimes. It just means I'm good at my work. And I am," she said, tilting her chin high.

He stared at her solemnly, and then he smiled. "I believe you. And I think I do see…a little," he said, staring at the roses. But now, with her admission and his, the room really did seem too intimate.

"Anyway, I do have to get out into the field," she said. "I need to scout out some new locations for group photos." And if we leave, we can go somewhere public, she thought. Not a place infused with all the signs of love and marriage. It was probably the atmosphere of the shop that was making her look at Dell as some sort of a romantic figure. "But I don't want to push you," she added.

Dell grinned, those amber eyes lighting up. "Now there's something few people attempt with someone like me. So…go ahead. Push me," he ordered.

She blinked. And then she grinned. "All right."

Quickly she turned to go with Dell right behind her, but just before they opened the door, she thought of something and turned again. "Dell?"

He looked down at her, his face only inches from hers. "What?"

She swallowed. "My friends…I haven't told them about our trial marriage. I don't want them to know. There's pressure enough without everyone waiting to see what happens and…"

His jaw tightened. His look was grim. "You think it won't work?"

"No, it's not that." But, it was, partly. "The thing is that we've given ourselves a trial of two months. If our marriage doesn't work after that, I don't want anyone to blame you."

An incredulous look came over his face. "Are you telling me that you're protecting me from your friends?"

Regina didn't answer at first. The utter ridiculousness of the situation hit her. Dell was probably invulnerable to anything her friends might say, but that wasn't the point.

"This place," she said, indicating the building, "reeks of romance. We see it every day. I just don't want anyone to expect that with us. My friends worry, and if they see us together all the time and know what we've planned, they might think that I'll end up in the same situation I was in before, falling for a man who doesn't love me. I'm trying to prevent that from happening."

"All right," he said, and she could almost see the wheels turning in his head.

She thought back over her words and moaned. "I meant that I'm trying to prevent them from thinking I might be in danger. I'm not trying to prevent myself from falling in love with you."

For a second she thought he looked amused. She knew she was blushing.

"Because there's absolutely no danger of that ever happening," she continued, babbling on. "I've explained that before and I just don't want them to look at you with expectations. Our marriage is…private, don't you think?"

For a second the look he gave her was searing hot. She remembered how he had come to her on their wedding night. She swallowed.

"Absolutely. Private. What happens in our marriage stays in our marriage," he promised. "And, Regina?"

"Yes?" Her voice felt weak and too soft.

"Thank you for worrying even if it was completely

unnecessary. I'm glad that your friends care about you and that they've been there for you this year when I haven't been. But I'm here now."

Somehow she managed to nod.

"Now," he continued. "Where are you taking me?"

"Oh, no," she said. "You'll just write it down in your plan book, and this is a surprise. No plans. We're going to wander."

"You can do that? During the workday? Just wander off and not know where you're going?"

She wrinkled her nose at him. "Some days I can. Scouting locations is an important part of my job, and I won't be gone all day. I have an afternoon appointment. It's one I can't miss because we really can't afford to lose the account. Especially with so much on our plates these days." The shop had finally turned a corner after three years and was doing well, but the added expense of Julie's wedding was going to cost the Belles some of their not yet comfortable cushion.

"What do you mean? What's on your plate?"

Regina recognized the calculating look in her husband's eyes, and remembering his comment about giving her the best cameras, she realized that she had made a tactical error in hinting at the shop's financial obligations.

"Never mind," she told him.

"Never mind what?"

"You don't get to dress up as the rescue squad for me. You've already done your part. Marrying me was enough."

Dell frowned.

"And anyway," she told him. "Everything is just great. We've got plenty of business and we've recently snagged a very big client in Liz Vandiver."

"Liz Vandiver? Daughter of Ephraim Vandiver, one of the biggest, most temperamental asses in the corporate world?"

"Yes. Don't worry. Everything's fine. The Belles and I just have to provide them with a totally scrumptious wedding, something unique and elegant, and our reputation will be made. Pulling off this wedding will be a coup that will attract other lavish wedding parties."

A frown marred Dell's gorgeous forehead. "Be careful, though, all right? Ephraim's a jerk, a powerful jerk."

Regina turned to Dell right in front of his car. "There you go again. Trying to protect me from life. You can't do it, you know. Life just keeps doing what it's going to do. Besides, the Vandiver wedding is my problem, not yours. By the time it takes place, two months will have gone. If this doesn't work, you and I might already be…"

He placed two fingers across her lips, stopping her. "Shh," he said. "I'll bet the D word is never used in a place like this," he said. "There might be customers nearby."

"Then I guess you're turning out to be pretty useful as a husband," she whispered against his fingertips. "How did you know we didn't use that word?"

"I read it in an article a local paper did on the shop."

She groaned. "Not the one where they ran a picture of me looking like a wild woman with my hair all out of place? I'd been down on my hands and knees arranging a bride's dress when they came in."

"You looked artistic," he said.

"Oh, you *are* learning to be good at this husband stuff," she said. "Because I know that you're the only person who would have looked at that picture and called me artistic. Even the other Belles called me maniacal."

Her words made him smile and she couldn't help

smiling back in return. The movement made her mouth slide against his fingertips, creating a deliciously erotic sensation.

Regina fought not to let him see her reaction. She pulled back. "We'd better go. I have a lot planned for us today."

"Then let's go, my maniacal, artistic wife. Your wish is mine to obey."

But Regina didn't even want to think about wishes, because for a moment there she had wished that Dell would kiss her. What a crazy thought. Because this trial marriage was all about being practical and friendly. Kisses weren't part of the plan.

At least not yet.

CHAPTER FIVE

FOLLOWING Regina rather than leading left Dell out of his element, but that couldn't matter. In the short time he had spent with his wife at the shop he had learned a lot about her. Even nervous and uncomfortable, her enthusiasm for her subjects had come through. And her photos, ranging from classic black and white studies to a playful picture of a bride crushing her new husband to her by pulling on his lapels, were works of art.

Amazingly enough, he'd seen little of his wife's work during this past year. She had none hanging at home. No doubt she considered the mansion too austere. The only photos were somber portraits of dead O'Ryans. At least he assumed that was her reasoning. He didn't actually know how she felt about much, not even about her miscarriage.

Dell pushed away his black thoughts and turned them to the future. Two months wasn't a long time to get to know a stranger and to try to craft a working relationship from air. If they didn't suit…failure was a possibility. He frowned.

"Are you okay? This is probably boring you," Regina said, flinging out an arm. "But, of course you've been here already, haven't you? You're the quintessential Bostonian."

Dell shook his head, stopping her. "I'm sure I haven't seen things in quite the way you have," Dell said, looking at the sculptures placed outside the Quinn cafeteria at the University of Massachusetts. The large pots and kettles looked like comic figures in a play.

"I love using sculpture as a backdrop for wedding parties. Here you have these sculpted figures with their slightly open lids, facing each other as if they're squabbling, and interspersed between them I get to place all these fabulously dressed and starry-eyed members of the wedding party who are so obviously bent on the harmony of beginning a new life together. Great contrast, and I think it might actually work, even though you can't hear the recording that accompanies the sculpture."

"Might be quirky," he agreed. "It might appeal to those looking for something different."

"I love different," she agreed, her eyes lighting up, and Dell just had to laugh. What would his parents have said if they'd been alive the day he brought her home? No need to wonder. They would have had plenty of criticism for anyone stepping outside the bounds of the conventional. They'd even be appalled at the way Regina eschewed traditional fashion.

She was practically dancing on her toes as she darted around looking at the sculpture from all angles. She was like tempting sunbeams, peeking out from the shadows of the sculpture and urging a man to see what lay underneath. The sun suddenly felt much more intense than it had only moments ago.

"Dell? Is something wrong? You're staring at me."

He'd never met anyone like her. The woman was practically electric. If he touched her…

Dell cleared his throat. "So you're a sculpture aficionado?" he said.

His mundane question must have reassured her. She took a shot of the kettle. "Oh, yes. It's big, it's bold, it makes a statement. What's not to like?" she said with a laugh. "But don't let me drag you around. You're free to go, you know."

"Trying to get rid of me, Regina?"

She blushed. In fact, Dell thought, he might have said it just because he had known she would blush and he was fascinated by the way it transformed her face into something out of the ordinary.

"No, but are you sure you want to be here? You're not just humoring me?"

"My choice," he insisted.

"No Chicago meetings?"

"Later."

"No major social events?"

"Not today, although there are some things coming up." He studied her. "In fact, I'd like it if you would accompany me."

"Oh boy, you don't really want me to put in an appearance at one of your social functions?" She sounded a bit breathless. Dell watched her with interest.

"I do. Will that be a problem?"

She considered it, practically wincing. "I'm not sure I would show well with the kind of people you're used to socializing with. I'm not exactly…"

He took her hand. "You're my wife, Regina O'Ryan, and you show quite well from my viewpoint." Too well. He was having to force himself to keep his hands off her, even though he knew that wasn't at all what she had meant.

"But…"

"Shh," he said, stopping her for the second time that day. "Don't criticize my wife. It's not allowed. She's rumored to have some very good friends who wouldn't like it, and neither would I," he teased.

She opened her mouth, then closed it again. "I don't think you were quite this bossy when you were young. At least you didn't seem like it from what I could tell the few times I saw you."

"You're right," he said. "I wasn't like this. I changed."

"What changed you?"

"My family. There were expectations. The O'Ryan heir must take charge. He has to be bold and forceful," he said.

"Well, you are," she said quietly.

"Yes, I am, I think. But, as I said, I don't want to push *you* around."

She shook her head. "You're not. We both agreed to try this and I knew that would mean occasionally being out of my element. So, yes, I can do wifely, I suppose. Just don't expect elegance. I wasn't bred to it."

"I'm not worried," he said, but he could see that *she* was.

As they continued on their tour of local sculpture, she barely spoke. Standing on the arched blue metal waves of the sculpted walkway at Constitution Beach, Dell watched her. He had said he wanted this marriage to work, but…what if it didn't? As a businessman, he'd learned to be prepared for all possibilities. Taking Regina into his world would be a good move on both counts. If their marriage worked, she would already have been introduced to his world, and if she still wanted

a divorce when the two months were up—he frowned—
well, knowing influential people would be good for her,
business-wise. Their patronage would help set her
business on solid ground.

"There's a charity ball in two weeks," he said.
"Would you go with me?"

"A ball?" She croaked out the words.

He chuckled. "Yes, you know the kind where you
dress up and there's lots of dancing and conversation?
They're considered pleasurable by some people."

But not by her, he could tell. Panic was written in her
eyes.

"Not a problem," she told him. "I'll be there."

"Spoken like a woman scheduled for a chat with the
Spanish Inquisition," he said lightly and with a smile.
"Don't worry. I'll stay right by your side."

But if anything, that only made her look more
panicked. Dell had to face facts. There was something
about him that made his wife uncomfortable. What was
he going to do about that?

Regina stared at the dress lying on the bed. It had been
two weeks since Dell had told her that he'd like her to
attend the ball with him. The good part was that he had
spent a lot of time in Chicago scouting out locations for
his new store so that she didn't have to worry about him
noticing that she found him attractive. The bad news was
that because he had been away she hadn't been able to
chicken out. It hardly seemed fair to leave him in the
lurch after she had already agreed to go.

Besides, she wasn't backing out now. During the
time they had been married Dell had asked nothing of
her. That article about Dell and Elise had only dredged

up the things that people must have been saying about him all year long, the things that Regina had, in her confusion and grief after losing her baby, been unaware of. Dell had no doubt appeared at numerous social functions this past year. It was part of his job and his heritage. People must have wondered what kind of wife he had married. They might even have questioned him as to why she was never at his side.

That must have bothered him. When he had talked about the O'Ryan expectations yesterday, she was sure he was merely scraping the surface. He was a prominent figure. As a married man his wife should have been with him.

Regina let out a long, deep sigh. "I'll be there tonight," she said. But she wasn't sure her being there wouldn't be worse than her not being there.

When she'd told her friends that, Audra had scowled. "That just doesn't make sense. You know how to talk to people. You do it every day in the shop. You deal with customers who have money."

"Yes, but that's just it. They're customers. I'm providing a service. These people tonight will expect an equal. I don't want them to think less of Dell for marrying—"

"If you say a nobody, I'm going to have to shake you, hon," Belle had said. "There's nothing at all wrong with you. I'm sure Dell doesn't think you're deficient, either."

Thinking about that conversation now, Regina sat down on the bed and pulled on stockings. She reached for the dress. *Dell thinks I'm a responsibility.* He had matched her up with his cousin, thinking he was helping the two of them. Then, when things hadn't worked out, he had become her rescuer. Now she had the feeling that she had become his obligation, his next O'Ryan project.

He had married her and, darn it, he was going to make a go of the marriage, no matter what. Defeat was not an option for an O'Ryan.

And she, fool that she was, had agreed to go along with the whole thing. Two months, he'd said, and most of that time was still ahead. They were supposed to be getting to know each other, but…

"I'm afraid," she finally admitted out loud. Dell didn't want love, *she* didn't want love, but Dell was a very potent man. He was hard to ignore. Despite her goal of a friendly arrangement, his presence made her think ridiculous, giddy thoughts. Lately she'd awakened from dreams of wedding nights…and heat, satin sheets, a man's strong, naked chest, things that went on in the dark between a man and a woman and…

"Agh! Stop it," she ordered herself. This trial marriage was purely practical and quite possibly temporary, and sleeping with a man who might be gone in two months would only complicate matters in dangerous, emotional ways. Hadn't she learned her lesson?

Yes. And what she knew was that she had better stop letting her thoughts fly off to fantasyland and start being the kind of logical, exemplary, helpful wife a man like Dell had a right to expect. Right now.

She took a deep breath and concentrated, but what she heard was her parents' voices. Try to be the right kind of wife tonight, Regina. Try to change who you are, try to be more like our friends' children, try to pretend you're not different. Try to finally make us proud and be a credit.

But later when she looked in the mirror, she didn't feel like a credit. The dress, an ivory strapless affair, looked elegant enough on its own. But her too ample curves at the bust and hip turned elegance into something more earthy, possibly even crude. She just hoped she didn't jiggle out of the top of the dress.

Or drop food on the skirt or laugh too loud or...

"Just stop it and go," she muttered to herself as she fastened on her own worst nightmare—strappy spiked heels she was forcing herself to wear but that she was afraid she wouldn't be able to walk in. Still, they were on her feet and they looked good. Slowly she moved out of the room and to the head of the stairs.

Dell stood at the bottom of the stairs and watched Regina descend. Out of her usual eyebrow-raising, bright-colored but practical flats, she was a bit awkward, tottering on heels. He should have told her she didn't have to subject herself to such torture, but when she lifted her dress to negotiate a step and he caught a flash of exposed ankle and leg, heat pooled in his body. The pale, slender dress and the shoes were the epitome of elegance, but Regina's lush curves and long, shapely legs gave her attire a highly sensual tone. Some might even say there was something erotic about her appearance.

And if anyone even hints that to Regina, there's going to be hell to pay, Dell decided. She had not wanted to come tonight. She was only here at his behest, and he would be damned if he would allow anyone to make her feel uncomfortable.

He smiled and held out his arm as she reached the bottom of the stairs. "You look lovely," he told her. Immediately he saw that it was the wrong thing to say, but he didn't know why.

"It's just me," she said softly. "You don't have to be *The O'Ryan* with me or say all the expected things. Time enough for that when we get there."

He growled. The woman had actually induced him to growl. Him. Dell O'Ryan.

"You *do* look very nice," he said, toning it down a bit.

She patted his arm as they moved forward. "I have a very clear full-length mirror, Dell, and the truth is that I look a bit like a stripper trying to play at being a duchess."

Dell stopped in his tracks and looked down at her.

"But a really nice stripper," she said, amending her comment. "And don't worry. I won't use the word stripper at the ball. I hardly ever use it at the shop anymore." She opened her eyes wide, feigning innocence, and Dell couldn't help laughing.

But despite her attempt to lighten the mood, Dell could see that she was still very nervous. He wanted to tell her to just be herself, but he was afraid of what would happen if she did that. Like it or not, he had been raised to a crowd that punished those who didn't follow the rules.

"I won't embarrass you," she promised.

"I'm not worried," he assured her, taking both her hands in one of his. And he *wasn't* worried about her behavior. What he was worried about was whether anyone would say something hurtful to her.

Regina had grown up only a few blocks from him, but it might as well have been a different universe. She was from a blue collar crowd where survival and financial security often depended on living by one's wits, and where the rules changed from day to day. He was from a slightly inbred group where the rules had barely changed in his entire life. Presentation was all, so when his mother broke his father's heart right after their wedding, that had been ignored. When she had cheated on her husband, she was ostracized by him in private but smiled at by him in public. The truth was that his kind sometimes ate their young if they didn't conform to the mold or learn the rules, Dell admitted. He couldn't imagine what they would do to someone like Regina. She roamed the streets with her camera and asked people about things few woman of this group would even admit to knowing, but she didn't know the secret born-into-wealth handshake. She had no knowledge of the rules that had been drummed into people of his ilk.

Still, if she could keep her secrets and charm this crowd, they would accept her as his wife. And later, even if she chose to give up being his wife, doors could open for her, and that was a good thing, too. If they stayed together when their two months were up, they would be on companionable and convenient terms and if they parted…well, he wouldn't have to worry that she would be inconvenienced or shunned. Her business, which meant so much to her, would thrive if she made connections tonight. So yes, there was a great deal riding on tonight, but there was no way he was going to tell her so.

"Just relax, and let the games begin, Mrs. O'Ryan," he said.

"Relax. Okay," she agreed, taking a deep breath that lifted her bodice and made his body tighten. Tamping down the sudden taste of desire was so difficult that Dell almost saw stars and he once again doubted the intelligence of his decision to do this, but then she smiled up at him innocently and nodded.

"All right, I'm ready," she said. It was so obvious that she knew she was going into the lion's den and that she considered this far more stressful than wandering the tougher areas of Boston. It was also clear that she believed she was doing this for him. Could he do any less for her?

He held out his arm and she wrapped her palm around it. Dell drew her forward into the night. They were strangers, and yet, tonight, they were companions on an adventure of sorts.

It had damned well better be a good experience and a rewarding adventure for her, he warned himself.

The room was all gold and cream and sparkling chandeliers with women swishing by in their long, tasteful gowns on the arms of men clad in severe black tuxes. A small orchestra played in the background, the champagne was flowing, jewels glittered in the women's upswept hair. Some of those women looked at Dell and gave Regina speculative or even evil glances as they passed. She tried not to squeeze his arm or cower. She hoped she didn't trip in these dratted shoes or breathe in too deeply and split the seams of her gown.

"I'd like you to meet my wife, Regina," Dell was saying, presenting her to a short balding man and his statuesque wife, the Nedlinsons.

Regina dipped her head. "I'm very pleased to meet you," she said, politely.

"Edward is in shipping," Dell explained. "He and Mary have three daughters in their twenties. Regina is in the bridal business. She's a wonderful and imaginative photographer," he continued.

Mary smiled. "It's so difficult to find a good photographer. Do you do portraits as well as weddings?"

A small bell went off in Regina's head as she answered the question. She was beginning to see why Dell had insisted on coming to her shop to learn about what she did. He was doing what might have been called "bringing her out" in another time and place. Once again, he was being responsible for her.

Part of her subconscious told her she shouldn't let him do this. She was capable of standing on her own two feet and even if they stayed married she still needed to do that. She could never be one of those wives who relied on their husbands to take all the responsibility for the family's future, but Mrs. Nedlinson was being so nice that it would have been rude to turn away from the introduction.

"I have to say I was surprised when Dell got married," Edward was saying. "We all thought—" He stopped midsentence and looked at his wife as if she had pinched him. Maybe she had because soon after that, Edward and Mary moved on.

"They seemed very friendly," she offered, thinking that she should say something positive. She looked up, right into Dell's intense amber gaze.

"Yes. They're some of the friendliest," he told her. And they had those three daughters in their twenties, she remembered. Marriageable age. Of course. Now she understood that Dell was handpicking the people he was introducing her to. They had to be kind and they had to be potential clients for her business.

This scenario was repeated over and over again with Dell's polite introductions, the other couple's equally polite responses and Regina struggling to maintain an air of worldliness she didn't actually feel. Everyone was on their best behavior, but she could sense their underlying curiosity. "How did you and Dell meet?" one woman finally asked.

"I just showed up on his doorstep one day," she said instantly, then realized how strange that sounded. "With his mail. I was delivering his mail," she explained.

The woman in question frowned, and Regina realized what she was thinking. "I wasn't his postal carrier," she clarified. "Not that there's anything at all wrong with postal carriers." She was beginning to babble.

"Regina and I were neighbors," Dell said gently.

Under normal circumstances that might have sufficed, but Regina could see the wheels turning in the woman's consciousness. Dell's house was magnificent and historic, but the O'Ryan mansion was an island unto itself. Sitting on several acres of land, the rest of the more elegant neighborhood surrounding it had been sold off and rebuilt. Consequently his palatial estate, once neighbor to other estates of its ilk, now sat in the center of a very blue collar area, its wrought-iron fence a barrier that had separated the O'Ryans from the riffraff.

"A neighbor," the woman said. "I see." And what she saw, Regina knew, was that Dell had married beneath him.

"But she's no longer a neighbor," Dell was saying, and there was a trace of dark, warning fire in his eyes. "Regina is my wife. She's an O'Ryan now."

And that was that, it was clear. Regina saw the startled look in the woman's eyes...and the acceptance. The great Dell O'Ryan had spoken. Arguments were futile, but she doubted that the woman had changed her mind about anything. In fact, Dell's insistence that everyone climb on board the respect-my-wife train had probably only verified what the woman already believed. Regina was a lowly beetle trying to mingle with the butterflies.

Dell instantly realized the futility of his comment. He might as well have announced that Regina was no longer a money grubbing opportunist. But there was little to be done about that now. Trying to explain any further would only make it look as if they were trying to hide something.

Besides, he knew the rules. This was a crowd where position had to be earned, even if a person had married into the group. One was accepted either with the passing of time or through action. But time wasn't an option, because if he didn't make this work in the next two months, Regina would move on. She would insist on going. He would no longer have the right to protect her. Tonight he had insisted she come here, but what if she ended up getting hurt from this encounter?

The very possibility made him angry…at himself and at his world. Now Dell was even more determined to protect Regina from harm, even though this wasn't achieving his goal. If he scowled at anyone, that wasn't going to help Regina. It was a dilemma.

She plucked at his sleeve and he looked down at her. "Great party, huh?" she asked with a too bright smile. "You know, I'm really starting to enjoy myself."

Not knowing whether to howl with frustration or laugh at Regina's obvious attempt to soothe him and convince him that she was fine with all this, he chose to smile. "I shouldn't have brought you here."

She stilled. Then she lifted her chin. "You know, if you were here without me, I'll bet you would be off chatting it up with the guys, talking major business deals or sports or whatever it is that you wealthy, old money types talk about. You should go do that. Now."

He blinked. "I'm not leaving you."

"No, really," she said. "I'll be fine. And I promise not to say anything too embarrassing. I do know how to conduct myself in public, you know. I do it every day."

"Of course. I know that." But he didn't want to leave

her alone. He didn't trust people not to attempt to weasel information out of her.

"And you're looking a bit bearish. People are going to think that we really must have some pretty big secrets to hide. Or maybe even that we've been fighting."

Okay, she was right...or maybe she just wanted to be rid of him. He couldn't quite blame her. The fact that he had dragged her to such a stuffy formal occasion as her initiation into his world, even if his intentions had been good, nagged at him. It was a bit like throwing a fluffy little lamb into a bunch of hungry wolves and asking the lamb to just try to fit in.

"You're sure you want this?" he asked, gazing at her intently.

She lifted those long lashes and stared straight at him. "I'll be fine. I promise not to hand out business cards or tell rude jokes or be ungrammatical."

He chuckled. "You wouldn't be the only person handing out business cards. Half the people here are making deals."

She wrinkled her nose and smiled. "Then I'll be on the lookout for promising subjects. Or I'll at least think of everyone as a photo op. It's pretty much what I do anyway. Don't worry. I'm not even nervous anymore."

No, she was tired of him hanging around her as if she might do something embarrassing, Dell could see. Or maybe she was just tired of him hanging around her.

"If you're sure," he said.

"I am. Have fun." She gave him a cute little wave and he reluctantly moved off.

He just hoped he was doing the right thing.

CHAPTER SIX

REGINA was petrified. This ball and these people…she was so out of her element. But she'd had to ask Dell to go. The more people had come up to check her out, the more he had looked like some delicious dark guard trying to protect her from snotty comments.

He'd been nearly irresistible. It had gotten so bad that the thought of trying to converse with people she had absolutely nothing in common with was less daunting than the sensation of standing next to Dell. She wasn't used to having anyone look out for her well-being, and she certainly wasn't used to being near a man like Dell. He made her want things she had no hope of attaining. In that respect this whole plan was probably unwise, but Dell had been so good to her and she had agreed to this trial period. She could at least make an attempt to fit in and be a credit to him. He probably hadn't known he'd married such a social misfit on their wedding day, but she knew that he would have gone through with the ceremony even if he had known. So, darn it, for once she was going to follow the rules and try to be something close to the type of wife Dell should have had. If he needed her to fit in here, she would fit in the best she could.

Just think of everyone as subjects, she told herself. *This is all one big session.* Dredging up a brilliant smile, she pushed her shoulders back, smoothed her hands down over the ivory silk of her dress and sallied forth to meet Dell's crowd.

She didn't even have to introduce herself. Apparently word had spread that Dell's wife was finally out in public with him, and the curious practically lined up to meet her. In a most polite way, of course. There were no lines. Everyone waited his or her turn. There was no pushing or shoving the way there was sometimes in the real world. No actual name calling. Maybe a sneer here or there, or a twitch, a shoulder raised haughtily or a cold tone. Eventually order prevailed.

Regina tilted her head. "How nice to meet you," she said to a woman whose name she immediately forgot. "Yes, I am a photographer. You would make a wonderful subject. You've got the perfect smile."

One down, she thought as the woman went away happy. Regina found Dell in the crowd and gave him a reassuring smile. He studied her as if he were checking for bruises and she shivered slightly. How could a man stare at a woman from twenty feet away and make her feel as if her clothes were too tight?

More people came by. She tilted her head, using her photo shoot technique to find the humanity behind the façade of each person. *A kind smile. Old, sad eyes. A wise expression. A jaw that would demonstrate a resolute personality. A face that would fade in group photos.* And while she took pretend photos she talked, just the way she did with her clients. "Tell me about your hobbies." "I'm afraid I haven't traveled all that much. Have you?" "You have a look in your eyes that makes me think you've lived an interesting life." "Your name is Angelique? I love that name! It's so exotic."

Between faces, she looked up to see that Dell had moved around the room engaging in discussions, but he was always turned toward her when she glanced his way. And he always looked up, straight into her eyes. The man had obviously learned the art of conversation as a baby. He could carry on his side of a discussion while staring at his wife as if he knew the intimate details of her conversation as well.

Sometimes Regina had a hard time looking away.

"A glass of champagne, madame?" a server asked her, holding out a tray.

"Oh. No. She might be pregnant," a silky feminine voice said, shooing the man away before Regina could tell him no, thank you. She hadn't been drinking tonight. A single glass could make her dizzy, but she liked the taste and occasionally drank socially or at dinner. It was a habit she'd cut out completely when she was pregnant, and tonight she had simply been concerned that if she used alcohol to brace herself, she might inadvertently say something that would embarrass Dell.

But this last decision that she shouldn't be drinking had not been her choice.

Regina looked at the woman. Slender, tall, blond, with eyes the shade of violets and a figure that was displayed to advantage in a peach halter gown that hugged her curves and displayed lots of perfect skin. In a most tasteful way, of course.

"Elise Allenby." The woman held out her hand. "You're Dell's current wife."

Regina felt as if she were suffocating. She resisted the urge to raise her eyebrows. Out of the corner of her eye she saw Dell and knew that he must have miscued in the conversation he was having because the man beside him stiffened and looked this way, too. She knew he was going to come over to attempt damage control, and she also knew that nothing good for Dell could come out of that kind of a scenario. As discreetly as she could, she gave a small shake of her head and hoped he understood.

"Yes, Dell and I are married," she said as airily as she could. Her earlier concerns about the woman's emotional state seemed to have flown out the window. With the words "current wife" Elise had signaled that she wanted a catfight. She wanted Dell and she didn't like the fact that Regina had him.

But I might not have him long if things don't work out, Regina thought. And in that case Elise might be Dell's "current wife" by this time next year. *So, smile,* she told herself. *Be nice. Do it for Dell.*

"I'm sorry. I probably shouldn't have made that comment about you being pregnant," Elise said. "I'm sure you know that Dell never was the type to like kids."

Touché, Regina thought, even as her heart cracked painfully at the thought of the child she had lost. Someone must have told Elise that she had been pregnant on her wedding day. Had it been Dell? If she knew that Regina had been pregnant, she must also realize that she hadn't had a baby. The coldness of her comments seeped in, making it difficult for Regina to even think or breathe.

But "No, I'm not pregnant," she somehow managed. Was it true what Elise had said about Dell not wanting kids? And yet he had married her because she was pregnant. If what this woman had said was true then he had sacrificed more than Regina had realized in order to marry her.

"I'm sorry to slip up on you in this sudden way. I know we haven't met, but I'm an old friend of Dell's," Elise was saying, her voice turning from harsh to slightly choked. "I've known him a long time. A very long time." And then Elise's face seemed to transform. She stopped speaking. She blinked. A look of horror came over her. She blinked again, and a tear ran down those beautiful cheeks, leaving a dark streak of mascara. "I'm sorry," she said. "I'm sorry I'm being so intrusive and mean and disgusting and crudely emotional."

Ah, she loved him after all, and she was horribly jealous.

So, despite Elise's harshness a moment ago, a part of Regina felt guilty. Had Dell given Elise up for the sake of a pregnant woman and an unborn child? Maybe not entirely, since he'd been raised to protect the family name and divorcing his wife so soon after marrying would certainly raise some eyebrows. But if their trial marriage failed and he wanted to marry Elise…

"Don't worry," Regina said softly. "You haven't hurt me." *If I'm hurting, I'm completely responsible for everything myself.* "Come on. I'll walk you to the ladies' room and you can repair your makeup."

Immediately Elise touched her hands to her face. "My makeup. Oh, as if I haven't been idiotic enough." She turned to flee, just as a very pregnant woman in a gorgeous gold gown came up to her.

"Elise! It's been so long since I've seen you," the woman said.

Elise shook her head. "Not now. Change of plans,"

she croaked. She rushed off, blotting at her cheek with a handkerchief she had pulled from the tiny bag she was carrying.

The very pregnant woman and Regina were left standing alone. The woman looked at Regina as if she wasn't quite sure what to say or do, but all Regina could do was stare at the woman's clearly pregnant state. She looked as if she should have delivered the baby yesterday. While Regina watched, the woman's belly undulated, a small lump making a gliding motion beneath the surface of the gold of her gown as the baby moved.

An arrow of hot, sharp pain shot through Regina. She felt achy and faint and frightened at the intensity of her emotions.

Change of plans, Elise had said. This meeting had been deliberate and cruel.

Regina struggled for breath. She felt rather than saw people looking their way. No wonder, with Elise the former almost-fiancée rushing away from the "current wife" with a tearstained face. Dell's friends were watching. Decorum was necessary.

Struggling to somehow smile just a little, Regina lifted her eyes to the woman's beautiful face. "I'm Regina O'Ryan," she said. "How wonderful about your baby. Will it be soon?"

Was that wrong? Was it a faux pas to ask about a woman's pregnancy when she was so clearly on the verge of delivering a child any second? Regina couldn't think. Memories and hopes and dreams kept pushing at her.

And words. Dell wasn't the type to want children, but he had married her. She wasn't what he'd wanted. Her baby wasn't what he'd wanted. Duty was all. He was the epitome of what this group stood for.

But he had been good to her. So good. She had to reciprocate.

"I hope I'm not being too bold or making you uncomfortable," she said, hoping her voice was strong and her expression friendly. "I'm just…children are so special."

The woman smiled gently. "I'm lucky," she said. "Thank you for asking. I'm Tonya Deerfield. And…I'm sorry." She touched Regina's arm just as Dell came striding up to them.

He gave the woman a strained smile and a curt nod. "Tonya," he said. "Excuse us. The dancing is beginning. I'd like to dance with my wife."

"Of course. Very nice meeting you, Regina," she said, moving away.

Dell said nothing. He simply took her hand and started leading her toward the ballroom. She was aware of whispers as they passed. It was clear that Elise's emotional exit had been witnessed by a large number of people.

"I'm sorry," she said.

Dell's steps faltered and she in turn stumbled slightly. She would have fallen if he hadn't swept his arm around her waist and steadied her. The iron strength of him and the warmth of his palm made her shiver.

"We'll talk later," he said, his voice low and tight. He was obviously angry. Her heart sank. None of this might be her fault, but she had told him she wouldn't embarrass him and now everyone was talking. She should have moved away when Elise approached her, she realized now. Who would have blamed her? But it was too late now.

"Smile," Dell said as he looked down at her and swept her into the dance. He, in turn, gave her a look that, under other circumstances and with another man, would have made her think that she was the most important person in his life.

He was pretending. Could she do any less? She smiled as brightly as she was able. And she did her best to dance, although the darn shoes kept betraying her.

Her heel turned, but Dell lifted her, bringing her closer to him, his chest nearly touching hers.

Regina's head began to spin at his nearness. She struggled for breath and hoped he didn't realize how he was affecting her. He was her former neighbor, her friend, not her lover or her love, despite their legal connection. She had to remember that. She and Dell were married but not in the usual sense. Still, she had promised to give this relationship, platonic though it might be, a chance. How could she do less when Dell had given her security and the opportunity of a normal life after Lee had deserted her? Taking a breath, she made more of an effort to stay upright.

"Look at me, not at your feet, Regina," Dell ordered, and she did. She gazed right up into his fierce eyes and found her balance.

Her gown was thin, and the warmth of his hand at her waist felt like a caress against her skin. But it wasn't. This was just a dance. This was how it was done. Dell had danced with hundreds of women just like this before.

Still, she didn't allow herself to look away. She smiled up at him, her gaze linked with his. For a moment, she forgot that other people were watching. For the space of a dance, the world held only her and this man who was keeping her upright by the sheer force of his personality. Her heart beat more strongly, her senses were heightened. She was so close to him that she could rise on her toes and kiss him if she wanted.

That thought caught her off guard. Emotion seeped

in, but…emotion wasn't part of this marriage, was it? Dell didn't want that. Of course he didn't, and it would be totally unfair of her to inject that element now. She had to look away from him, and only with great effort did she maintain her balance. But the music was ending. The dance was over.

"It's time to leave," he said.

She understood. Now they would talk. And it would not be good.

The ride home was silent and strained. Dell didn't trust himself to speak. Because once he began to talk, all the emotions that had been roiling through him tonight might come out, and it wasn't safe driving with that much explosive energy blowing up in both their faces.

So he tried not to think about how small and tense Regina seemed on the far side of the passenger seat. She was almost wedged up against the door.

No wonder. He must look like a thundercloud. He was certainly feeling like one. And the storm was about to hit.

Somehow, someway, he got them home. He handed Regina out of the car and led her to the door.

He opened it and followed her inside, sliding the lock into place behind them. The outside light's glow filtering through the fanlight window cast an eerie shimmer of pale yellow light framed by dark shadows in the high-ceilinged entranceway.

Regina held herself rigid, almost as if she were waiting for him to strike. And then she did a very brave thing. She turned and faced him.

"I shouldn't have gone there," she said.

"I shouldn't have made you go," he countered.

"I told you I could handle myself, but speaking to Elise was a foolish move. I...I guess I wasn't thinking straight."

Dell wanted to laugh, but it would have been an ugly, harsh and sarcastic laugh. *He* hadn't been thinking straight for a very long time. Certainly not tonight.

"Do you really think I believe any of this is your fault? Regina, I as good as pushed you into that appearance. I didn't even stop to think that Elise might be there."

"Do you think *I* believe that you would do anything that would intentionally hurt her?" Regina asked.

Dell scowled. "Of course not, Regina. You wouldn't hurt anyone. I led you into a risky situation and then left you there alone to fend for yourself."

"I'm not spineless or helpless. You know that. I made you go away and leave me alone at the ball. It was my decision."

Now, he did smile. He couldn't help himself. "Regina, do you really think you could make me do anything I didn't want to do?"

A look of intense concentration came over her face, wrinkling her nose in a delightful way. "All right then, I *asked* you to go."

Ah, she had him there. He had left her side tonight because she had asked him to. "Maybe that's true, but if I had known you would be subjected to Elise Allenby, the meeting would never have taken place."

"Dell, you can't stand between me and life. You've already done that. Elise said you didn't want children."

"Did she now?"

"So you sacrificed yourself by marrying me."

"Really?" He seemed less than convinced. "The ranking O'Ryan needs an heir."

She blinked. "Oh. Yes. So, are you actually trying to

tell me you married me because I was pregnant and you needed an heir?"

No, he'd been trying to bluff.

"How *do* you feel about children?" she demanded.

"I don't know much of them." He sidestepped the question. Obviously not adroitly enough. He saw the accusation in her eyes. It was valid, too. He knew nothing of children, and given the fact that he was too much like his father, he doubted that he would be good with them. Still, he knew Regina would have been good with children. And the child she had been carrying…

"I might not have been the best choice for your child's father, Regina, but I would have welcomed your baby. In the end, I wanted to see your child born. I wanted to be a father." His voice cracked on the words. He tried not to think back to the day when he had come home to find her as pale as winter snow and as silent. She had allowed him to take her to the doctor and then she had retreated. So had he. "I—your child would never have been a burden or an obligation," he said, "if that's what you were thinking."

And just like that, those pretty brown eyes filled. She closed her eyes and swayed slightly. He caught her, his palms closing around her arms, her skin yielding beneath his touch.

He felt her tremble. He breathed in her scent and desire swept through him. Unfair. He couldn't treat her this way, not after all the pain his actions had caused her. It wasn't her fault that he was having trouble controlling his reactions.

And yet, he was having *so* much trouble.

"Regina." She opened her eyes.

He slid his hands beneath her hair. "Promise me…" He pulled her closer.

"What?" she whispered, looking up into his eyes. Such warm caramel eyes.

"Taking you to the ball this evening put you at risk. Promise me you won't let me nudge you into any more situations where you'll feel uncomfortable." And he knew as he held her here that he wasn't just talking about events like this evening.

"I won't," she said.

"I mean it. Don't do something just because you think I want it or because you think it's part of our plan. If I'm out of line, in any way, if you feel I'm pushing you, I want you to push back."

He took her hands and placed them palm down on his chest as if to demonstrate.

Big mistake. The warmth of her hands resting against him was too much. Slick desire coursed through him. He placed his palms on the curve of her waist, his actions belying his words. Her dress was thin. She felt so right. And soft. In just a second, if he didn't stop, he would crush her to him. He would taste her, push her, break his promise about not touching her before their two months were up and again risk rushing her into something she might not really want.

Dell ordered himself to step away completely.

Regina stared at him as if she had known what had been going through his mind.

"If I do that again, I want you to stop me. Tell me no," he said.

She raised her eyes to his and said nothing.

He groaned. "Regina. Please."

She nodded hard. "Yes. I will. I'll stop you. Next time."

The words "next time" hung between them like a threat. Like a promise.

He slugged in a deep breath of air, trying to pull it together. "Good. I think…good night." It was time to get away before he changed his mind and touched her again.

He turned, headed toward the stairs.

"Dell?" Her soft, sad voice stopped him cold and he turned back to her. He waited.

"You didn't hurt me tonight. It was difficult talking to Elise, but I have to learn how to handle those kinds of situations. I need to be strong. No, I *am* strong."

"I know. And you handled it well, but that doesn't mean I would ever drag you through something like that again." And then because she looked so small and alone and pretty, he smiled.

And got a tremulous smile in return for his efforts.

"Sleep tight," she said.

As if that was going to happen. Tonight he had done what he had never considered doing since the night they had wed. He had touched his wife.

It couldn't happen again. At least not yet. If this relationship was ever to be forged, it had to be built on steel, on trust. It had to be proven to be something that could last, not a thing of heat and passion that might die out and leave only ashes and the need to dissolve their union as quickly as possible.

He would not be just another man taking advantage of her warmth and her giving ways, he would not follow the path his cousin had taken with Regina. Only when she had decided that she could be his partner forever would he allow himself to claim her body.

CHAPTER SEVEN

REGINA was jumpy and tense at work the next day. No question why. She was lusting after her husband.

Please don't do something stupid, Regina, she told herself.

But it was too late. She and Dell had overstepped the bounds last night. There had been touching. Not just platonic touching, either. She knew that as well as she knew that her heart was hammering out of her chest. He had wanted her.

And oh my, she had wanted him. The longing had been deep and strong and almost overwhelming. It was a wonder that she hadn't pressed up against him. She had almost not been able to stop herself.

Thank goodness he at least had stopped, because she had a bad feeling that physical contact between them might lead to longing on her part and that was just...so wrong. If she started wanting more than Dell was offering, she would get seriously hurt.

"Regina?"

Regina looked up, confused.

Belle was staring at her. "Are you all right?"

Giving herself a mental shake, Regina nodded. "I'm perfect. Why?"

"You've been staring at the appointment book for three minutes. Was there something you wanted to record?"

Trying to remember, Regina finally frowned. "Yes, the Vandivers want to expand the number of places where I'll be taking photos. An engagement party, two showers, a bachelor and bachelorette party as well as a complete pictorial of the entire day from the time the bride and groom arise to the time they leave for their honeymoon. They want everything bigger and better. We're to spare no expense."

Regina felt a brief moment of panic. "I'll have to hire another photographer for the separate locations, but I suppose that won't be a problem. It can't be. What the Vandivers want, the Vandivers get, right?" She looked at her friends.

"Right," Natalie said. "I got a call, too. More tiers on the cake and an expanded dessert table for those who don't want cake. I'm sure I can do this. I'm even working on a special cake. I'll need all of you to taste it, so get those taste buds in gear. You're all so good at making helpful suggestions." But she sounded a little flustered herself and it wasn't just the fact that Natalie was diabetic and had to have her friends do her cake tasting. That was part of her everyday existence. The Vandivers were being more than unusually demanding.

Regina looked toward her other friends. "Anything else?"

"Lots more beads on the dresses," Serena said. "All the dresses."

"Flower arrangements for every location they visit on the wedding day." Callie smiled tightly. "And for special guests. There are quite a few special guests."

"We're going to have to ask for a bigger deposit,

Belle." Audra looked worried. "Extra people and materials are going to stretch our budget. I mean, we'll get it all back the day of the wedding, but we might have to be careful until that day."

"I don't want anyone having to beg Liz Vandiver for money," Julie said suddenly. "She's being disagreeable enough as it is and changing her plans five times a day. You can just…I don't want the Belles to go under because you're spending money on my wedding."

Everyone froze. "How did you know?" Audra asked.

Julie looked around the room. "None of you are very good at keeping things from me. All those furtive looks you've been exchanging. Besides, I found some notes that had fallen next to a trash can when I was emptying it yesterday. It must have been from a brainstorming session you were all having. I'm not going to let you sacrifice anything for me."

Regina forgot her own problems. "Julie, we're fine. Your wedding to Matt is a gift to ourselves as well as you. We love planning every detail. Don't make me tell you this again. We have money, and we're using it. You're going to have the perfect wedding and marry the perfect man. Okay, sweetie?"

Julie's eyes teared up. "I love all of you so much."

"We love you, too, darlin', so don't worry about the Vandivers," Belle said. "They're pompous, but they know business and they know that when they want something extra, it costs. I'll handle them and I'll be so delightfully charming they'll fall over their feet to throw bushels of money at us."

Finally Regina smiled. "You're always charming, Belle. That's why everyone loves you. By the way, Rae

Anne called. She wanted to know if Charlie Wiley had come in to see you."

Instantly Belle frowned. "I wish she would stop trying to fix me up. Charlie Wiley called yesterday while I was out, but I'm not interested in another new man trying to frisk me. If he comes in or calls again you can tell him that."

Immediately everyone looked a bit uncomfortable. "That wouldn't feel right, Belle," Julie said.

"I know. I'm just mad. I'll tell him myself. Now, you girls get going. Isn't it your weekly poker night?"

It was. But Regina couldn't do it. Yesterday evening was too much on her mind. If she socialized with her friends tonight, she didn't trust herself not to open up and relate her fears. And if she went home…

She couldn't go home yet. Not until she'd had time to work off some of her fears and inhibitions and get back on track. Today's crop of sparkling-eyed brides hadn't helped. She needed something rougher. A good dose of reality.

"I'm sorry guys. I have work to do," she said, grabbing her camera bag. "If I'm lucky I can catch Edna before she goes to work."

"Regina…"

Regina whirled around, walking backward toward the door. "You know I hate missing poker night, but I have to."

"And you know that's not what Audra is worried about," Callie said.

"I know, but there's no need. Edna's a good person."

"I'm sure she is, but…"

Regina smiled and waved. "I love you guys, and I appreciate your concern, but there's absolutely no reason for you to worry," she said. And she hurried out the door.

Of course, she was wrong. There was a lot to worry about. Mainly how she was going to keep from thinking about the way Dell's hands had felt against her skin and how she was going to manage to pretend she hadn't felt a thing. The time until the end of this trial period seemed longer than ever.

Dell hung up the phone and swore. That had been Belle.

"Dell, I wouldn't have called under normal circumstances. This feels a bit like a betrayal, and my concerns are probably unfounded. It's most likely just me doing that mother hen thing, but Regina's gone out on a photo shoot and…I don't know. She's used this woman and place as a subject before, but she doesn't ever miss the girls' poker night for something like this. Besides, this time she seemed a bit distracted," the woman had said. "I'm sure the neighborhood's fine if a person is with someone, but alone…a woman needs to stay alert. Regina doesn't like anyone going with her because she says it breaks the trust of her subjects, but if you could just keep a distance, make sure she's all right and give me a call when you get back, I'd really appreciate it."

His temper had started to rise. "She shouldn't be going anywhere even remotely questionable. Couldn't you stop her?"

Silence had ensued. "Regina is an adult. She's a professional and she's exceptionally good at what she does. She's also smart and fiercely independent and she needs to be that way. So if you're going to lecture her or treat her like a child I'll look elsewhere. That girl has had enough lecturing to last her a lifetime. Her parents did it every day of her life, and some of the men she's known—"

He swore and ran a hand through his hair. "No

lectures. But I have to know she's safe. Can you give me an address?"

"I can give you an area. It's all I know."

But when she had named the region, Dell blanched. "I'm gone," he said.

"You'll call?"

"When I deal with my anger."

"Dell…"

"I'm her husband, Belle. I have a right to be angry."

"If you hurt her…"

"Never. She's always safe with me. I promise you that. You'll just have to trust me." He didn't wait for an answer. In ten seconds flat he was out of the door and headed into one of the few dubious areas of the city. He had no idea what he was going to say to Regina when he found her. Somehow, he hoped he would find the right words.

The best of the light was starting to fade when Regina peeked out from behind her camera and noticed that Edna was staring at a point somewhere behind Regina's shoulder. The woman was frowning.

"What are you looking at?" Regina asked. "Is something wrong?"

"Time for you to be going, I think, sweet pea," Edna said. "There's a man sneaking about. A pretty young thing like you shouldn't be here at this hour. I tried to tell you that earlier."

"I know, but I had time today, and I wanted to finish your part of the story. You're so unique, Edna. Thank you for taking the time with me."

The older woman nodded. "You're always welcome, Regina, but now you really need to be going. I don't like this at all." An edge crept into Edna's voice.

Regina's heart began to pound a bit. With the late summer sun it wasn't even close to dark but she was usually here only during the busy part of the daytime. Now the streets were becoming deserted, and if there was trouble...

"I'm not leaving you to fend for yourself," Regina said.

The woman cackled. "Honey, I've been fending for myself all my life."

And she had paid a high price many times, Regina knew. "I'm not leaving. We'll go somewhere else. I'll call the police if I have to." But she knew Edna wouldn't want her to do that unless she really had to. There were good people in this neighborhood who nonetheless had shady pasts.

Still, when two men started walking toward them from the other direction Regina's heart fled into her throat.

Edna growled. "Look out. Here comes trouble. You go home now."

"Edna," one of the men called. "Who you got there with you? She's pretty."

"She's nobody," Edna said. "Get out of here."

"Oh, no. I don't think so," the man said, continuing to advance. "I want a better look. Maybe a taste. I definitely want me some of this."

"You don't want none of this," Edna said. "She's sick."

"You're lying. I can tell. That woman is soft and stacked and—"

"And she's most definitely mine," a low, deep voice announced, and Edna's eyes widened. Regina whirled to see Dell walking toward them, fire in his eyes. "Furthermore, if you come even one step closer to her, I will hurt you beyond repair," he promised the man.

The man hooted. "With what? You got a gun?"

"Much better than that. I've got a cold, hard direct line to the police chief on my cell. He's an old friend. If you want to meet him just take one step closer to my wife."

"Wife?"

"Absolutely." He pulled out his cell, flipped it open and pressed a couple of buttons. "What is the closest intersection? Oh, yes," he said, naming the two nearest streets. "What are your names?" he asked the men.

"Yeah, like we're gonna tell you that."

"That's Bodie and Reg," Edna said. "I can tell you where you can find them most of the time, too."

A slow, lethal smile turned Dell's grim expression into a dark mask of satisfaction. Someone must have answered the phone. "I've got a situation here I need an assist on," he told the person on the other line. "Good. How long? Ten minutes? Make it five."

One of the men let loose a string of curses. The two of them started to back away. "We're gone, man. Never even saw your woman. She's safe. Got a hands-off perimeter around her."

"Yeah, that's right. It'd be real smart to go home right around now, Bodie," Edna said.

"Shut up, old woman. You and me will meet later," Bodie said, but he pulled the other man away and together they retreated down the street.

Regina looked up at her husband, who was canceling his order. He wasn't looking any more cheerful. She raised her chin and took a deep, shivery breath.

"I—Edna, I'd—I'd like you to meet my husband," she said, turning toward the woman. No one was there.

"She slipped around the corner," Dell said.

"You scared her away."

"I don't think she was scared. Not of me."

He was most likely right. Edna wasn't scared of much, and the look in her eyes when she'd realized that Dell was Regina's husband had been much closer to admiration than fear. Knowing that, Regina felt a deep sense of relief slide slowly through her. Bodie had scared her. She wasn't going to admit it.

"Maybe she wasn't exactly scared, but Edna wouldn't want to meet the police chief any more than those two men would," she explained. "She has…a background."

"And this neighborhood isn't the safest, yet you're here. Without adequate protection." His voice was low and soft and disappointed. It was worse than having her parents chastise her, even though no true words of criticism had left his lips.

"Edna's special," Regina explained. "There are those here who have hard lives. Now that she's old and not able to work anymore she helps those who need it. She takes care of them when they're sick. She runs errands. She writes letters for runaways so their families won't worry."

"She could let their families know where they are."

"If she thought it was right, she would. Every case is different. Edna is different."

He was advancing, still with that look of utter frustration on his face.

"Damn it, Regina, *you're* different. I don't want you hurt on my watch."

The words sank in. *On his watch.* A finite period. He was conceding that this marriage might not work. She gave a quick nod. "I know. I'm sorry. I just…"

He shook his head. "Don't explain. I know this is your work, your life. I know how important it is, but…"

She waited.

He blew out a breath. "I can't be the way you are. I have to know you're safe."

There was an edge in his voice but also a note of defeat. Pain bit at Regina. She had broken trust today and all because she was trying to stay away from home to protect her heart.

Giving a quick nod, she moved a step closer. "Remember how I said that I hoped we could be friends eventually? I still feel that way, and friends don't ignore friends' concerns. Today, someone had to have called you. That means I worried the Belles. You, too. That's not right. I—" She tried to find the words.

"I'm not asking you to give up your work, Regina. I would never do that, but I can hire people to come here with you."

She gave a tight nod. That would never work, but it would probably only be for a short while.

"Good people," he amended, watching her. "I can afford the best. Former Navy Seals, the top detectives in the country, people who know how to disappear into the brickwork. They won't interfere unless you're in danger."

Gratitude filled her soul. She fought the hot tears that threatened. "Thank you," she said.

"Let's go home," he said, holding out his hand.

And though touching him was even more of a danger than Bodie had been, Regina took his hand.

CHAPTER EIGHT

Two nights later, Regina lay in bed staring at the ceiling, the memory of Dell walking toward her saying "She's most definitely mine," in a continuous replay, and every time that deep baritone sounded in her memory, she shivered with awareness. Her husband was a very commanding, very physical man. He had ridden to her rescue no questions asked when Belle had called.

For the moment it didn't even matter that he considered her an obligation, a bit of family duty. At least, she wasn't going to let it matter.

Dell had saved her skin. What's more, he had most likely saved Edna's. She knew because she'd received a phone call from Edna today.

"Guess where I am?" Edna had asked. "I'm on the street, talking into my bodyguard's cell phone. Isn't that a hoot?" she asked with a trill of laughter. "Me, Edna Dooney, with her very own personal bodyguard to keep the Bodies away. Doesn't talk much, but he's sure handy at carrying things and frowning. You tell your man thank you, all right? You sure got lucky, girl."

"Yes, I sure got lucky," Regina whispered in the

dark. Dell was rock solid, a good man. He had helped her so much.

And what had she done for him? Other than bringing him his mail one day and giving Lee enough confidence to disappear off on his own personal quest?

"Not a thing," she muttered. "What could I do for someone like Dell?" She'd been mulling over that question for two days. And she had no answer other than the subliminal *Sleep with him* that kept creeping into her thoughts.

"Just stop it!" She moaned, turning over. "That's not the way I want things to work." If they ever did sleep together, it had to be because they both wanted it and the time was right. What she wanted to do for Dell had to be different. Out of the ordinary.

She threw off the covers and paced the room. Flipping on her computer, she pulled up one of the few pictures she'd taken of Dell. He was turned to the side, his jawline a blade. The photo had been taken back when she'd been dating Lee, and Dell had been happy then. Less tense. He was smiling at something in the distance. He was…impressive, very aristocratic, very Boston.

Regina frowned at that. She clicked onto the Internet and typed Dell's name and the word Chicago into the search engine. One small page came up, the same passage she had mentioned to him that day she had asked for the divorce.

She typed in jewelry stores and Chicago and a host of them came up. Obviously Chicago was a competitive market. Despite the fact that there were those who wanted him to set up shop in the town, expanding there could still be a risk. A new enterprise would need to stand out from the crowd. A major public relations push would be necessary.

"Which Dell knows and which he can well afford," she whispered. No doubt he had the best agencies available at the task right now.

But they don't know him personally. They don't know what makes him tick, what makes him stand out as a man and what makes him interesting.

"You don't, either," Regina told herself. At least she didn't know enough to approach him with the idea that was forming in her head. But then she hadn't known Edna, either, at one time. Or Lyle, the doorman who serenaded the people in his apartment building. These people were Boston, Regina thought, opening up the files she'd made for the book that was almost completed.

And so is my husband. There's no one more Boston than he is, she thought, thinking of this old mansion and the weight of the history lining the walls in those old, somber photos of former O'Ryans.

Regina smiled. A plan swirled, began to take shape and solidified. "I think my book needs another chapter, maybe an excerpt that might be sent out as a teaser. Maybe even some people in Chicago might find that interesting."

She flicked the computer monitor off and lay back down, but she didn't go to sleep. It didn't matter. Excitement filled her soul. There was one thing she could give to her husband. It might be the last and only thing she ever did for him.

That thought stung, but she did her best to ignore it. Nothing, not even painful thoughts, were ever allowed to interfere with her work, and this was definitely work.

Her troubles with Dell were over. Now he was a subject, and that was so much easier than having him as the man she desired night and day.

* * *

Dell was pacing the floor of his office, his phone up against his ear when a knock sounded on the door. Since only he and Regina and a few servants occupied the house, Regina had left for work hours ago and the servants always waited until his door was open, there had to be something wrong. He tried not to remember how he'd felt the other day when he'd seen that jerk leering at Regina and holding out his hand as if he intended to touch her.

A muscle in Dell's cheek twitched and he quickly excused himself to the associate on the other end of the line, rounded his desk and reached the door in two strides. When he pulled it back, Regina was there. And so was Edna. His wife looked a bit guilty.

"I'm sorry if you were working," she said.

"Something's wrong. Bodie?" he asked Edna gently, turning to the woman who bore the scars of a hard life on her wrinkled face.

"No. Bodie tried to come around once and Samuel scared him away. That man you sent me is something," Edna assured him.

"I don't understand, then. Do you need something?" he asked.

But already Regina was slipping into his office. "Just a few minutes of your time, Dell. Hardly anything, really." She pulled out a camera that was the equivalent of a photographer's phallic symbol. Dell knew powerful men who would covet that camera. But, he thought, remembering the photos he'd seen on the walls of The Wedding Belles, they wouldn't be able to make use of it half as well as his wife did.

Then, as Regina began to set up, the reason for her visit hit him. "You want to take my picture? Why?"

His wife gave him a patient smile, although he

detected a slight shift to her eyes. Was she about to lie to him? "I told you about my pictorial of Boston. It's almost done. Edna and I are pretty much through, and I have lots of other Bostonians, the meat of the city, but…it occurred to me that I'm missing something. I have hardly any old school types, not many wealthy people and no blue-bloods to speak of. You could really round out the last chapter and help me sell the thing."

She was still smiling but not exactly looking at him. Interesting.

He glanced at Edna. "She wants to take our picture together, so she can have a caption about how you helped me," the woman told him.

Dell was taken aback. "Not necessary. That wasn't meant to curry favor with the public."

Now Regina had one hand on her hip and she was looking at him dead-on. "I know that, Dell, but putting something like that in a public record could help Edna and others as well. It might help raise awareness of those who have limited resources and might bring in donations. I intend to list a couple of organizations Edna has worked with which provide medical care and social services to the people who need them but are afraid to ask for them or can't afford them."

Her expression was earnest. He fully believed she meant what she said and he knew she cared about Edna, but…

"You already have a segment on Edna."

Ah, the evasive look again. "But not one of someone like you who can actually help. Besides, you're making this move to Chicago. If I send out some complimentary copies to the right people, it could be a bridge between the two cities. For Edna, I mean. That is…people might mail in donations even from that far away."

A smile played at his lips. "Edna doesn't look too bothered by the lack of donations flowing in from Chicago." He looked at the woman. She shrugged.

Regina's shoulders slumped. "You've hardly said anything about the Chicago connection. Some targeted publicity would be a good thing for you and your business, wouldn't it?"

Undoubtedly, but he wasn't concerned about his slow start. He'd held off on some things so that he could concentrate on his marriage. "I'm not worried about Chicago," he told his wife.

That seemed to worry her even more. "See, you're taking care of the rest of us, fussing over me and not tending to your own needs."

He chuckled. "Regina, relax. I'm not going to go broke."

Uh-oh, now she had that offended look in her pretty brown eyes. "Do you think I don't know that, Dell? Heavens, you must have more money than—I don't know—pretty much anyone I know. That makes it really hard to do things for you."

Her meaning became even clearer. Dell tilted his head. "Does it matter? Doing things for me?" A slow thread of interest wound its way through him. Was there more to this marriage than he had thought? He studied his wife carefully.

"Yes," she said as if that didn't make her happy. "You've done so many things for me. What have I done for you?"

Answers flowed into his consciousness. She'd brought the element of charming surprise into his life but he knew from experience that Regina considered her tendency to do the unexpected a detriment. She'd shown him how important a smile and compassion could be, but again, he didn't think she would believe him if he told her that. And besides, he wanted her closer than this when he whispered that to her. He wanted to be touching her, and they weren't alone right now.

"You married me," he said simply, and that, too, was obviously the wrong response. He could see that she wanted to counter his suggestion, but with Edna in the room she probably didn't want to go into details.

"I want to do something real and meaningful," she said, clearly unhappy. "To use my skills. Dell, I need to contribute and I haven't. I can't clean your house or help you in your work or…anything. I can't save you from the bad guys and the bad parts of life the way you did me. Let me do *something*. I'm a really good photographer."

"You're the best. I've seen some of your work," he agreed. And if he didn't let her do this, he would be devaluing her talent. "What do you need me to do?"

Instantly that miracle smile lit up, bathing her face in pure, beautiful seductive light. "Just let me shadow you a bit, ask questions, take some pictures. We would have to be…together a fair amount."

"Yes," he answered immediately, and he knew it wasn't the pictures or the interviews he was saying yes to. In spite of their plan for a trial marriage, they had danced around each other, even avoided each other at times. Because there was such a strong urge to touch her, to make love with her. He knew that, and he knew that the choice to stay married or not to stay married couldn't be complicated by lust that might fade away in time. If they stayed together it had to be for solid reasons. Otherwise, like his mother who had withered away an unhappy woman, their marriage might destroy Regina. Or, like his father, who regretted marrying the wrong person every day of his life and took it out on others, the two of them might grow bitter. They would hate each other.

He never wanted Regina to hate him.

"Let's do it," he said again.

Regina grinned. "Edna, we're on," she said, but it was Dell she looked at with total excitement in her eyes.

Immediately his body tightened and desire filled him. Sometime soon, he promised himself, he was going to kiss his wife. Probably just as soon as he got her alone.

Talk about burning the candle at both ends! Regina had been rushing from the shop to Dell's side for three days. Where he was, she was, and she was amazed at some of the places her husband showed up at.

"The bird house at the zoo?" she'd asked, trailing her husband through the gates.

He'd laughed. "I know, but the client is a world famous ornithologist proposing to his lady love. The ring is a custom job and he insisted that I transport it myself. It's shaped like a rare hummingbird from Peru, one he's spent his life studying." He'd flipped open a ring box and Regina had stared down at the most exquisite little ring she had ever seen. Diamonds and sapphires and amethysts made up a perfect miniature bird nesting on a delicate gold band.

"It's beautiful," she'd said with awe. "You?"

He'd shaken his head. "I didn't design it. I just made it happen."

That was what he appeared to do, she realized the more she followed him around. He made things happen.

In the short few days since she had started this project, Dell had appeared at the mayor's office donating money for a green project several businessmen were sponsoring, he'd handled an emergency with his housekeeper, providing her with a car and driver, money and lots of reassurance so that she could visit her daughter who lived in Iowa and had delivered triplets three weeks early. He'd fielded calls from his office and soothed ruffled feathers when there had been a mix-up in accounting and his employees had been pointing fingers at each other. He was a man in control and on top of things at all times.

And today they were about to attend a late meeting followed by a cocktail party with his associates regarding the progress of the Chicago expansion.

"I'll just stay near the back," she whispered to him as they entered the room.

He smiled and slipped his arm through hers. "Be my wife tonight," he urged. "Not my biographer."

Regina glanced up into Dell's amber gaze. She needed to answer but her breath felt shaky. She realized that she'd spent days focusing on him, learning about him. It was all impressive, but she had been-mostly-able to lock it away in her mind as work. This would be different.

"I'm not dressed for this."

He glanced down at the plain, sleeveless black dress she was wearing. It was one she had owned years before she had met him and it was not O'Ryan quality. The other women in the room were suited and coiffed, perfumed, bejeweled and expensive.

"I look like someone you picked up at the discount

store," she said, intending to step away and hide behind her camera.

He smiled and her heart did that flippy thing it had been doing for three days. "Then I got a bargain," he said. "Even rich people appreciate bargains. There isn't a man in the room who hasn't given you an appreciative glance."

Okay, now she was out of her element. "I—you're kidding me. I—"

"I meant that as a compliment, Regina."

"I know." Her voice came out a bit mortified. "I don't handle compliments well."

He shrugged. "You don't have to say anything to me. With other people, a simple thank you will do."

She nodded. "Okay, what do you want me to do?"

"Be here. Next to me."

Oh my, she felt suddenly warm. "All right."

But within a few minutes of the presentation beginning she was fidgeting. She felt conspicuous. It was stupid, she knew, but she felt as if she needed a reason to be here and she didn't have one. She wasn't really a part of the company or of Dell's world.

"Mrs. O'Ryan," one man finally said, interrupting the procedures. "That's a gorgeous Hasselblad you're carrying," he said, pointing to her camera. "I understand you're a photographer. Why aren't you taking pictures?"

She opened her mouth, but didn't know what to say. Her fingers plucked at the camera, a familiar object she trusted. "I—" Regina turned to her husband, and a resigned smile of defeat came over his gorgeous features.

"She was just waiting until we were done with the boring part," he said, giving her an encouraging smile. "But I'm sure she'll take your picture now if you're nice to her. She *is* a very talented woman."

With a relieved grin, Regina turned to her husband and mouthed the words "thank you" just before she raised her camera. For the next forty-five minutes, she shot photo after photo, but found herself returning again and again to her husband. Here was Dell with a woman coated in diamonds; here he was with his arm reassuringly on the shoulder of a man wearing a worried look on his face.

"It's time to strike in Chicago," the man said. "If you delay any longer, you'll lose the opportunity. Already some of the people who were trying to coax you to come are moving along to the next new thing. They loved your rare creatures collection and the fact that you try to be socially responsible, but they're fickle. You need to make a move, find a location."

Regina took a photo, but she said nothing. She was listening intently, taking shot after shot of Dell. The look in his eyes, the deft way he handled the man's concerns, the very shape of his hand and the lines of his body were an aphrodisiac for her camera.

Soon she had forgotten what she was doing. In fact she had forgotten everything except making love to her husband with the camera. When she suddenly dropped to her knees and panned her camera upward, taking a series of shots ending with a close-up of his face, she heard a gasp behind her.

Immediately Regina was back in the here and now. She blinked, then frowned, wondering why everyone was staring at her. A woman came up behind her. "Dell, you could at least have leaped in here and done the honors," the woman said as she drew Regina up and draped an arm around her.

The movement upward revealed a flow of air over

Regina's back. "Oh my goodness," she said, realizing that the thin, aging fabric of her dress had given way with her athletic movements.

She glanced up at her husband, whose hooded gaze was fierce. "You're right, of course, Lisette. I should have been the one to tend to my wife."

And in one swift, graceful move he slid into place, replacing the woman, leading Regina toward the ladies room. Once inside the empty room, he whirled her around and pressed her up against the wall.

"I'm sorry," she said. "I'm so embarrassed. All your friends saw, and darn it, I wasn't even wearing my best underwear. Don't people always say to wear good underwear in case you have to go to the hospital? But this isn't the hospital. It's worse. The cream of Boston society saw my faded pink bra with the stretched out strap and the hole in the nylon and—"

"Shh," Dell said, and then his lips came down on hers.

Sensation claimed her. Dell's lips were magic. She was sinking, reeling, aching, mindless. She wanted more.

Her arms came up around his neck. She rose on her toes and angled closer.

When he finally released her and pulled back a bit for air, Regina blinked to get her bearings. "I'm so...I don't know," she said.

"Regina, you're driving me absolutely insane," he said. "You and your camera, all this concentration on me, all this closeness. Did you really take a picture of my pants?" He tilted his mouth over hers, caressing, licking, driving her mad.

"I—I might have," she said when she could speak again. "I don't know what I was doing. I wasn't thinking."

"Mmm." He kissed her again. He ran his hands up

her sides, and she shivered. Somewhere in the back of her mind a voice reminded her that a roomful of elite Bostonians had seen them come in here together and that she had been half-dressed.

Alarm bells rang in her head. She pushed at Dell.

Instantly he released her, although his hands were still lightly resting at her waist. "Dell, you're not thinking straight, either. That man was right. You're supposed to be working on Chicago, but you've stayed here because you feel some sort of obligation to me and our plan."

He frowned. He opened his mouth, no doubt to deny it. She placed her fingertips over his lips. "Admit it. You should be in Chicago."

He didn't say a word, and he didn't look happy.

And she knew the truth. For both of them. "Dell, you said I was making you insane. I feel the same way. I *have* been taking too many pictures of your body. I *am* lusting after you, if you couldn't tell. It's only natural. We're a man and a woman and we spend a lot of time together. But what's going on between us…it's lust," she said. "That's what was between Lee and me. Lust." Although it had never been like this. Nothing like this heat and need and fear of tipping over the edge. Fear of feeling more. "I don't want that to happen to me again," she whispered.

Immediately, without another word or touch, Dell removed his hands from her waist. He turned her around, reached for a bowl of safety pins kept on the counter and deftly pinned her dress closed.

"I'll go to Chicago," he told her. "I'll give us both a break."

When he turned her back to face him, she nodded.

He forced a smile. "But do not get rid of this dress. I love this dress," he told her.

Her own smile was tremulous. "Thank you," she whispered, and she knew that he understood that the thank you wasn't for the dress. It was for allowing her to save herself.

CHAPTER NINE

REGINA felt as if she had run Dell out of town. It was one thing to take pictures of the man. It was another to forget what she was doing behind the camera. If she hadn't been so pushy, she and Dell wouldn't have ended up in each other's arms, forgetting their surroundings, and he wouldn't have gone away.

The truth was that she missed having him around. Trying to fill her time so she wouldn't wonder how he was or what he was doing, she devoted herself to working on his section of the book. She cruised the Internet looking for background information on the O'Ryan empire and located an old box of O'Ryan family photos, a pitifully small collection. All of them were professionally done and painfully posed. No pictures of Dell with chocolate on his face or skinned knees. His smiles were television, public-eye smiles. Where was the real Dell?

Regina frowned. She chose several, then moved on to Dell's downtown store and office. Despite her "three days of Dell" as she was beginning to think of it, she still hadn't visited his offices. As she did for all appointments she called ahead, but even being married to

Dell she felt a vague discomfort explaining to the management just what she wanted to do. No doubt they couldn't be too careful when a place loaded with jewels was at risk, but a part of her wanted to keep saying, "I'm really his wife. It's okay for me to come down and take photos, isn't it?"

Instead she gritted her teeth and ignored the disapproving glances of the personnel when she finally showed up to take pictures of the lavish, gold and silver and white establishment that was a perfect backdrop for all the diamonds and rubies and emeralds. Her feet sank into the plush carpeting as she visited Dell's office and ran a finger over the massive mahogany desk that must have been in the family for generations.

"It's lovely," she told the frowning woman who had led her there.

"Of course," the woman said. "But, this is highly irregular, Mrs. O'Ryan. Mr. O'Ryan is not a rash man or one who does things without telling me. He sticks to a schedule, he comes to work precisely at nine and leaves precisely at five and he always gives me his agenda and his list of daily contacts."

Ouch! Clearly a wife wasn't on the list of today's contacts, Regina thought. She wondered if Dell had chosen Louella or if he had inherited her with the company. The woman's description of his life seemed so harsh and sterile, so devoid of fun or spontaneity.

"Dell won't mind," she said, hoping that it was so. He had always been kind to her and he had okayed her project. But then she had never invaded his workplace or messed with his agenda before and she hadn't informed him that she was coming here.

The woman frowned harder.

"Why don't you call him?" Regina asked.

"I already have. I also checked your background on the Internet, Mrs. O'Ryan, long before you married him. Doing background checks on all employees is part of my job."

Regina opened her eyes wide at the implication that she was no different than an employee. Darn. This woman thought she had married Dell for his money. Regina had a terrible urge to try to explain that money wasn't the issue here, but that would only have sounded pathetically conciliatory.

"Then everything is all right, I suppose," Regina said, brazening it out. Louella obviously didn't agree. She opened her mouth to speak just as Regina's eyes lit on a glass case in which an exquisite emerald necklace was displayed.

"Oh, my." Regina practically breathed the words. She had never really owned jewels, but she knew that these were out of the ordinary.

As if she had threatened to steal the woman's child, Dell's secretary moved to stand in front of the case, a human guard. "These have belonged to *the O'Ryan Bride* for the past five generations." Her implication couldn't have been clearer. Regina didn't rate. She had not been given the jewels.

But Regina wasn't offended. She wasn't really Dell's bride, and the tense pain that coursed through her had nothing to do with her need for the man. It simply reflected her regret that she would never understand a relationship so strong that it would inspire a man to want to give her such gems.

She smiled at the woman. "They're lovely."

Then she brazenly took a step to the side, raised her

camera and fired off a shot. She might never use this photo, she certainly would ask Dell's permission first, but for now she was married to *The O'Ryan* and she would not be treated as an interloper by anyone other than her husband. Only Dell had that right.

Thanking the woman, Regina took a few more photos and left. A sense of loss and loneliness overtook her. It was probably just because when she looked at the photos and at the text she had included so far, there was still something missing. She didn't know what, but she would have to keep following Dell until she got the magic element she needed.

That fact weighed heavily on her. Those comments she had made to him about lust had not been the whole story, either. The more she knew of her husband the more he fascinated her. Edna had contacted her and told her that she now had more helpers. Besides protecting her and some of her friends, they were making city gardens for the local residents, giving them access to healthier food and sunshine. All of this was, of course, Dell's doing. He felt that promoting his wife's causes was part of his duty. She was his responsibility. And yes, he was her fascination. But fascination, especially toward a man like Dell, could be dangerous to a woman's heart.

At home, she stood outside the door to the room he used as an office. She had been inside before but the details eluded her. It was the man who had caught her attention. She wanted to go inside, but…she had already gone too far. She wouldn't invade without him being here. As for entering his bedroom…

Regina closed her eyes. She had been inside. Once. The memory was a blur. So soon after Lee's humiliating desertion, she had been desperately unhappy and ashamed. She hadn't even really been aware who had been touching her when Dell had put his hands on her body. All she had felt was that she was a throwaway, a second best. She hadn't believed in Dell's passion and so she hadn't wanted it. But that was before these last few weeks, before she had gazed up into those fiery amber eyes, felt his heat, had his mouth cover hers and fill her with mindless desire.

"Mrs. O'Ryan?"

Regina raised her head and looked up to see Janice, one of the maids, staring at her with a concerned expression. She realized that she had stopped outside her husband's bedroom and that her forehead was resting against the wood. She was remembering Dell's scent and wishing that he were here.

An automatic urge to press her palms to her cheeks and scurry away, embarrassed, came over her. It was what she might have done a few weeks ago before the trial period had begun. But would an O'Ryan wife do something so pathetic?

Regina raised her head and gave Janice a big smile. "My husband is a compelling man, Janice. I miss him," she confessed.

And Regina realized that it was true, a distressing fact she refused to examine. If she was starting to miss him, a man who felt strong emotions were a serious mistake in a marriage…she couldn't complete the thought.

"It's good that you're feeling well enough to miss him, ma'am," Janice said. "I know you were sick for a while. Mr. O'Ryan told me you needed quiet and time to recover. I'm sure he's happy now that you're feeling so much better. I'm glad you're much improved, too," Janice added. "He's a good man and he deserves someone who cares."

The two of them exchanged a meaningful look. Dell was obviously of importance to both of them.

Regina knew then that this private woman-to-woman exchange wouldn't go any further. The maid wouldn't feel compelled to share this with Dell the way she would if she had thought her mistress was looking ill again.

A small sense of satisfaction filled Regina. She had taken a step closer to being something akin to a true O'Ryan bride who was beginning to feel comfortable in her adopted home.

Her satisfaction lasted until the morning when she went down to breakfast and found her husband sitting there.

There was a look in his eyes that seemed to see right through her clothes to her skin, even to her soul.

"You're…Dell, you're home," she stammered like an errant child caught in a fit of misbehavior.

His laugh was delicious and bold and sexy. Sitting there in his white shirt that showed off his tanned skin with the black pants that fit him to perfection, he looked like an unattainable piece of temptation. Man candy dangling before a woman who really needed to stick to her diet.

"I'm home. I hear you've been visiting."

Regina's jaw dropped. "Louella called you to tattle on me."

Dell's amber eyes gazed into her own. He grinned. "Louella is a tigress where my office is concerned."

"Tell me about it," Regina said. "She didn't want me there. But I'm not apologizing. I wasn't doing anything wrong."

"You're right," he agreed.

"And I was working on the chapter for the book. It's supposed to help you, not hurt you."

"I know that. I told her that."

"But you came back to check up on me."

Slowly he shook his head. "Not in the way you mean. I came back to reassure her, yes, and also because when I reprimand an employee I like it to be face-to-face."

Shock filled Regina's consciousness. "You don't have to reprimand her."

"You're my wife."

He had said that several times, but what did it mean? Regina knew. It was a matter of duty, of position, of protocol. She had married into the O'Ryan clan, taken the family name and that alone afforded her a certain measure of consequence. It had nothing to do with how he felt about her.

A slow ache surprised her. She forced it away.

"Don't reprimand her," she said. "Louella is prickly but she cares about you. I'm sure she thought she was protecting you."

"I'll be gentle," he promised. "But I won't have anyone criticizing my wife. Especially not my employees."

"She was probably worried that I was trying to use you or that I wanted your money. Besides, I don't want her to dislike me," she beseeched. "That would make our marriage more difficult."

He frowned and started to protect.

"Please," she said.

Dell blew out a breath. "All right, but only because you requested it."

Regina nodded. "I got the feeling Louella was, I don't know, rather maternal about you."

Immediately he looked wary. "I suppose she is. Most of the people who were around when my parents were alive tend to be that way."

It was one of the few personal things Dell had ever

told her about himself. He knew a lot about her background. She knew very little about his.

Without thought, she sat down at the table. "Are there very many of those people around now?"

Dell's hands folded around his coffee cup as he shook his head. "Most left during my father's last few years. He was…difficult. Partly I think it was the fact that he was ill, but he was also an intensely bitter man."

She wanted to ask why but that seemed intrusive, too nosy. "He seemed distant the few times I saw him when I was a child."

"He was. Always. That wasn't the illness or age." Then Dell reached across the table and took Regina's hand, lightly caressing her fingers. "My parents had an unfortunate marriage. My father fell head over heels for my mother when she was only nineteen. She was very beautiful, exotic, highly emotional and impulsive. He was rich. She became pregnant."

A deep sense of dread came over Regina. She struggled to battle her emotions.

"He married her, of course, and things should have been all right."

"But they weren't."

"No. Not at all. He loved her. But for her, he had merely been a lark, an impulse. Even worse, she fell in love with someone else—my father's valet. It was…ugly."

"Why didn't they divorce?"

"Pride. The desire to avoid scandal and…in the end, they made it work. It wasn't pretty but over time they developed a respect for each other."

"And you?"

He shrugged. "They pinned their hopes on me, that I would be smarter, handle things better."

And not get involved in a messy emotional relationship, Regina assumed. "And everyone else pinned their hopes on you, too? Louella?"

"As you said, she cares in her way. I've disappointed her before, so she's touchy."

Regina assumed that he was talking about a woman. That made breathing difficult, but she couldn't think about that. With great effort, she managed a smile. "Well, we'll have to prove to her that you're acting smart now."

But his gaze locked with hers. "I'm not sure I am."

What did that mean? Regina didn't know, but it was obvious that it wasn't making him happy. What would make him happy—or at least distract him?

"Edna sends her thanks. I think she's driving Sam nuts. He says she's giving him silly jobs."

He smiled. "Good. Sam needs to be less serious sometimes." But Dell still didn't look totally relaxed.

"Did something go wrong in Chicago?" she asked.

"Everything's fine," he assured her, but his response was too quick, too casual. Something was wrong.

"Are you going back after you speak to Louella?"

He slowly shook his head. "I would have had to come back in any case: When I spoke to Louella, she reminded me that I had appointments and obligations."

Regina nodded. She was pretty sure that some of those appointments and obligations were social. Yet he didn't request her presence. No doubt after the last fiasco, he had decided he would be better off without her help.

In the past, that might have been a relief. For some reason it wasn't today. Which was totally ridiculous. He *was* better off going without her.

"Well," she said, backing away. "It's good to see you."

"Off to work?"

"No. It's my day off. You?"

"Louella. Then work." He rose and came up behind her, putting his hands on her shoulders. "Thank you," he said.

Regina frowned. "For what?"

"For holding back and giving me the chance to have a heart-to-heart with Louella this time. But I intend to let her know that you have full access to the office and make it clear that as my wife, you have the right to do as you please. And in the future, don't be afraid to speak your mind."

She grinned. "I didn't. I took a picture of the bride emeralds, even though she didn't want me to."

"The bride emeralds?"

"Yes. You know the ones."

His hands tightened on her shoulders. "I should have already given them to you."

"No. You shouldn't. It's a love gesture. That's so not us. And besides, I might be gone soon. You have to keep the emeralds in case there's another Mrs. O'Ryan."

Silence settled into the room.

Dell's hands loosened slightly on her shoulders, and Regina thought he was going to let her go and leave the room. Then he bent nearer, swept her hair back and kissed her neck. So lightly his lips barely made contact.

But she felt it. So deeply. With a shiver of anticipation and desire.

"I'll see you later," he whispered as he whisked out of the room. It was a simple statement, the kind people make all the time to the most casual of acquaintances.

But Regina's heart began to racket around in her chest with an eagerness for him. That was regrettable. She couldn't start needing to see him all the time or someday she would be the one he was reprimanding and explaining things to. Things like "don't expect love. That's not what this is about."

But at least you already knew that, she thought. At least you can insulate your heart.

And at least for today she wouldn't have to worry. It was her day off and she had plans that didn't involve having to steel herself against desiring her husband.

CHAPTER TEN

HE WAS supposed to be staying away from his wife today, Dell reminded himself. This was her day off and she was probably looking forward to some alone time, free of the restrictions of being his wife.

He frowned, thinking of how uncomfortable she had been at that gathering last week and how shabbily his office staff had treated her. It was a reminder that not all women were dying to be Mrs. Dell O'Ryan. The truth was that if this kind of thing kept up, Regina might be happier without him. He should give her another day off before they tried again.

Yes, here he was walking into the garden. He stopped just inside the gates. Regina was down on her hands and knees pulling out a weed next to a white petunia. She hadn't seen him. There was still time to be smart and retreat. But there was also that old line about meeting challenges head-on. He and Regina had been apart for days, and time was passing. If they continued keeping their distance, where would they be when this trial was over?

He drew nearer to his wife. "I have gardeners to do that."

No startled look. All right, she had obviously already realized he was here.

"Yes, I know you do," she said, "but I talked Fred into letting me have my own little plot of land. I like gardening. Callie's been teaching me some stuff."

She liked gardening. He had been married to her for almost a year, so why did he not know that?

"Show me," he said suddenly. He dropped to one knee beside her.

"Dell, your pants. You're not dressed for this."

"They're only pants, Regina." The soap clean scent of her invaded his senses.

"Only pants. They're probably designer or something like that."

They were an exclusive Italian brand. But she didn't have to know that, and it wasn't important. His clothes were expensive but they were just clothes. They were replaceable, not like time missed with a woman who might decide to leave soon. In that moment, his decision about whether to stay or go to the office was made.

"Stop complaining about my pants and show me what you're doing," he teased. "Maybe you can teach me something and I can impress Fred with my extensive knowledge of soil types. The man has considered me a hopeless case ever since I rode through his prize rosebush with my bicycle when I was twelve."

Finally she laughed. It was such a lovely, unfettered sound that he couldn't help moving closer. "I'm just tending them so they can keep growing, and there's not much to say. These are simple gerbera daisies, nothing exotic," she said, moving to another mound of bright pink, white and yellow flowers. "But they still need to breathe. It just takes some simple get-your-hands-dirty work."

He leaned closer and plucked out a weed, his body close to hers, the warmth of the sun and her nearness incredibly soothing and…something else. Exciting? "You think I can't get my hands dirty, do you, Mrs. O'Ryan?" he asked, trying to keep his tone light.

She waved her hand airily. "*You're* an O'Ryan and as you mentioned, you grew up with gardeners to handle the messy stuff."

And she hadn't. It occurred to him that despite their proximity he had little experience of the world she'd grown up in. Whatever had happened to her had made her strong, but she was fragile, too. And, he reminded himself, for the time being, at least, she was still his.

"It's your day off," he remarked. "Are you going to spend all of it in the garden?"

She turned toward him and now her face was only inches from his. "No." And for a second he wasn't sure if she was telling him not to get any ideas and lean closer or if she was answering his question.

"Care to elaborate?"

"I have plans. Not gardening plans."

Okay, this was his cue to leave. She wasn't volunteering what she was going to do, so she obviously didn't want him to know. Maybe there was even a man involved.

"Mind if I tag along and shadow you?" he asked, to his own and obviously to her surprise as well. Those caramel eyes opened wide. She seemed incapable of speech.

"But then, I might be intruding," he offered. "In which case, I'll withdraw that suggestion. Pretty rude of me anyway."

"No." She paused. "I mean, no, you aren't being rude and you wouldn't be intruding. I just, well, of course you can come. We're supposed to be getting to know each other. I want us to be friends. And after all, I've spent plenty of time following you with my camera. Fair is fair."

Which meant she really didn't want him along but she was going to put up with him.

Dell felt a slight sense of annoyance…and a decent measure of satisfaction.

"It's part of our trial period, part of the plan, after all," she added.

His satisfaction faded. He was beginning to be tired of the plan as the main reason for their every interaction. But then it was, wasn't it? If he hadn't insisted on a two-month trial to try to save their marriage, she would have already filed for divorce. Perhaps he should have let her do that.

"Regina, maybe—if I forced all this togetherness on you, you can say no to more of it."

She rose to her feet suddenly. "Is that what you want?"

"No, but I don't want you to be unhappy or to feel trapped."

"Then we'll go on," she said, raising her chin in a haughty, pretty way. "I think…we're making progress, and besides, I have plans of my own. I want to write your section of my book."

All right, so he was a subject now. Someone she could photograph. Irritating as it was, he could live with that, he supposed.

"I'll meet you back here in twenty minutes, all right?" she said, moving toward the house. "Wear something you can burn later."

And with that intriguing comment, she left him. There was a spring in her step. Dell realized that that was a new touch. Just two weeks ago, she hadn't looked nearly so perky. And now his wife got all excited at the prospect of using him for a pictorial subject and also at the prospect of getting dirty.

A chuckle slipped between Dell's lips. He took the stairs two at a time.

"You call those casual clothes?" Regina asked, eyeing Dell's obviously expensive and pressed khakis.

"They'll burn as well as any I've got."

She sighed. "You're probably right. It would be too much to expect an O'Ryan to have blue jeans in his closet."

"I have them. They're nicer than these."

"Let me rephrase that. It would be too much to ask to expect an O'Ryan to have *normal* blue jeans in his closet. Like these," she said, pointing toward her own well-worn jeans with a hole in the knee and another enticing place high on her thigh where a few remaining strands of denim crossed her pale skin, revealing more than they covered. The jeans fit her as if they had been made to her exact measurements, cradling a slender waist and the flare of her full hips.

"Very nice," he said, his voice thick. He couldn't help examining that bit of naked skin at her thigh.

"Come on," she said, blushing as she turned and showed him her delicious backside. "I'll drive."

Dell groaned.

"Hey, I'm a good driver," she said.

"You are," he admitted. "I've seen you drive. But I'm a tall man."

She studied the little red subcompact. "I love my little car."

And what was he to do? He folded himself inside. Now they were in this tiny space together. His knees were jammed to his chest. His head was against the ceiling. And his arm was almost touching hers. Suddenly the car seemed much nicer.

Regina looked at his pretzeled body. "Oh, you poor man. What am I thinking? You're right. We should take your car."

"No. I'm good." He turned and looked at her and realized that he really was good. She looked perfect in the car. It made her happy.

"You're not good. Your poor knees." She leaned closer to get a view of his position and her body brushed his thigh.

Oh, yes, he was very good. He had an ache, a physical ache, one he couldn't assuage without being a jerk. But that was his own problem.

"Drive, Regina. I'm fine."

"All right. It's not far." But she didn't tell him where they were going.

"You might change your mind, and now that I have you, I've decided to use you."

Interesting. He stared at her.

She blushed. "Your muscle power," she explained.

Even more interesting. "You'll see," she added lamely.

But he still didn't understand when she pulled up in front of the local animal shelter.

"Muscle power?" he asked.

"I take pictures of them," she explained. "Sometimes they're rambunctious. There aren't enough volunteers and the animals aren't used to so much individual attention. And if there's someone who can hold them and pet them while I take the shots, it's easier to make them look cute and lovable and help them find homes."

Her voice was matter-of-fact, but he could see by her

expression that there was nothing matter-of-fact about her reaction. And once inside he saw even more evidence of how much this meant to her.

"Hello, Maynard," she said to a little Airedale with a body that wriggled uncontrollably when he saw Regina. "Still here, sweetie? He has issues," she told Dell.

"Issues?"

"He was mistreated by his owners. Can you imagine? Who would hurt a creature with eyes like this?" she asked, her soul in her own eyes.

He *could* imagine. She had been hurt, and he knew that. It killed him that people—Lee—had hurt her, but…had he been any better? Lately he had been asking himself how he could have been married to her and known so little of her.

She looked up at him and now she was wary. "Don't do that," she said. "Don't look that way."

"How am I looking?"

Regina glanced away. "Like there's something about me that makes you feel guilty. All the time."

"No. That's not how I feel about you all the time." But he wasn't sure what he did feel. Barely controlled lust of late. But he wasn't about to tell her that.

And anyway, just then Maynard whimpered. Regina bent over the little creature and stroked his wriggling body. "I'm going to do my best to find a place for you, Maynard," she said. "A safe place. I'm going to make some lists of possible owners. I'll be like Dell here. You'll be part of my big plan."

When she looked up, she was wearing an impish smile.

"Are you teasing me, Regina?"

"Yes, but you're an O'Ryan. Teasing is probably bred out of you."

"Maynard, the woman is incorrigible," Dell said. "I hadn't realized."

She laughed. "Come on, Mr. O'Ryan, we have work to do."

For the next several hours, she put Dell through his paces. "Yes, hold him just like that. You look good with a dog. Oh, yeah, this man is going to sell you to the public, Phoebe," she told a flirtatious white poodle. "Women will take one look at him holding you and say, 'I have to get me some of that.'"

"Phoebe, I feel exploited. I'm nothing to this woman but a backdrop."

"A sexy backdrop," Regina insisted.

"Well, that makes it so much better," he agreed, and actually it did. He was having the time of his life. Regina was in love with these poor creatures so in need of a home.

"They haven't measured up. In some way they've all been considered deficient," she explained later when they were on the way home, tired and wrinkled and with tears in their clothing where dog and cat claws had occasionally broken through. A black lab named Sandy had been especially enthusiastic about meeting Dell and had bowled him over, ripping his shirt and giving him a tongue washing.

"You were good with them," she said. "Thank you. I was teasing earlier but it really could make a difference to have you in the shots. I want them all to be saved, to find good homes, and frankly, I don't care if it takes a gorgeous man in the picture to do the trick."

Her tone was so fervent, so poignant that Dell couldn't look away from her. A sudden thought came to him. His cousin Lee had been a lot like a lost puppy.

"Were you trying to save Lee?"

The sudden change in topic and the personal nature of the question had been unfair, Dell conceded. Regina's hands tightened on the wheel. She went silent for five whole seconds. "No," she finally said, her voice not much more than a whisper. "I don't think so."

"I was."

She nodded. "Why? He was an adult."

They were just outside the gates to the house now. Regina stopped the car and turned to look at him. As if she didn't trust his words to be true and had to see his expression.

Dell held out his hands in a dismissive gesture. "Lee was an adult but he came to live with us as a broken child. His father, my uncle Jack, had been wild and rebellious, and my grandfather had disinherited him. Jack married a woman just as rebellious. It wasn't a good relationship, and they were abusive parents, I think. By the time they overdosed and Lee came to live with us, he was nervous and awkward and a bit wild himself.

"Still, we were cousins, and I grew to care about him. My father was impatient with him. He never felt that Lee could represent the family in a good light and he didn't mince words. I became Lee's protector. I tried to teach him things so that he wouldn't make my father angry. Lee wanted to be accepted in the worst way. He always told me that he wished he were a true O'Ryan."

"Wasn't he?"

"Of course. But my father wouldn't let him forget that his parents had created a scandal. Lee wanted to escape that bad boy image so much."

"So you tried to help him become a true O'Ryan." Regina's brow furrowed. "Was I a part of that plan, then?"

"At some point you *were* the plan. Nothing else had worked."

She shook her head. "I don't understand. I don't meet any of the O'Ryan requirements. I was never a debutante."

The more she spoke the more Dell realized how much he had wronged her, used her. Not that he hadn't already flayed himself with that whip when Lee had deserted her. "A debutante would have been more of what Lee had been handed all his life. He wouldn't have met expectations; he would have been hit with criticism. Not because he lacked breeding or money. What he lacked was confidence. He needed kindness, someone who would give him stability, stroke his ego, make him less anxious and help him come into his own."

"And I was to do that for him?"

"Yes." His answer was terse. "I didn't know he would hurt you, Regina. It never occurred to me that that might happen."

He gazed into those clear, kind eyes of hers and found that she was looking back at him, full of pride, her chin held high. No tears, no accusation in her expression.

"I knew that you thought I would be good for Lee. Why else would you have introduced us? But I never knew you expected me to be able to do so much, that you had that much faith in my abilities. And see, you were wrong. I didn't do any of the things you thought that I could. I failed."

A rush of anger and frustration rose up in Dell. He leaned across the small confines of the car and reached out. Sliding his fingers into Regina's hair, her cupped her face, staring down into her eyes.

"Regina, you didn't fail. I was unfair, and I am so incredibly sorry."

She was shaking her head. "Don't be. I was old enough to know what I was doing. I got sucked in."

"Because you loved him, and I let that happen."

Gazing up at him, she stared directly into his eyes. He could feel her pulse beneath his fingertips. "I don't think I did love him. That is, I cared about him immensely and I just…you're right. He was like a puppy, and that kind of wide-eyed loyalty and neediness can be very appealing."

Her lips were so close, so full, her words so soft.

Dell swallowed. "Do you still miss him?"

"I only miss what I thought he was, and…"

"What?" His voice was a harsh whisper.

"I love the fact that you cared about him so much, that you wanted to help him fit in so he wouldn't be hurt."

"Don't make me out to be the good guy. I was raised to follow my duty, to know what a good O'Ryan should be. That was my goal, to turn Lee into a good O'Ryan."

But that look in her eyes, those luminous, lovely eyes…

He leaned closer and covered her lips with his own. He tasted her fully, deeply, sipping at her lips. She was soft, giving, sweet and moist. Desire spiraled, and he pulled her closer, his palms skimming down her arms to her waist.

Regina shifted and slid her long fingers into his hair. She kissed him back.

He leaned into her touch, bending her backward.

The small, shrill horn of the little car went off as they leaned too close. Dell jerked and banged his elbow against the dash.

Regina shrieked.

The sound of voices sent them both turning. There were people across the street taking pictures. Not of them but of the estate. It wasn't unusual. The house was on the

National Register of Historic Places, and sightseers were fairly common. What wasn't common was him making out with his wife in broad daylight in a too small car.

Not that he minded. At all.

His wife clearly did. "Dell," she whispered in his ear, urgently, pushing at him. "Dell, people are watching us."

"Not us. The house."

"But we're here. If they take a picture and you're in it, sooner or later, someone might notice that it's you...and me."

"We're married."

"I don't feel married right now."

Something hot and fierce lanced through him. He pulled back and stared at her. She didn't seem to notice. "I feel like some teenager having sex for the first time in the back of a car."

Which only made Dell more aware that he hadn't yet made love to his wife. At least not fully. And he wanted to badly. Right now.

"What would we say if they recognized you?"

"Regina, not everyone knows who I am. They're just interested in the house."

But the group was coming closer. "I feel conspicuous," Regina said. "I'm going inside."

Without another word she got out of the car and started toward the house. *What was a man to do?* Dell thought. He followed his wife.

"Excuse me," one member of the tourist group said. "Do you know anything about this house? Who lives here?"

Dell watched as a very pretty blush climbed his wife's cheeks. "The O'Ryans live here."

The people shook their heads as if they didn't know

the name. They probably didn't, and, bored, would leave soon, move on to the next mansion.

But to his surprise, Regina suddenly looked indignant. "Of the O'Ryan Gemstone Galleries? They make jewelry for the stars."

Now the group was interested. "Do you two know them?" one man asked, indicating the path Regina was taking.

His wife looked delightfully flustered. Dell held back a grin.

"No," she said suddenly. "That is, not personally. I just—clean their house and my husband, Donald, is the gardener. He weeds the flower beds."

"So…you get to see the inside?"

"Every day," she assured them, but Dell couldn't help noticing the tension around Regina's eyes.

"Well, it's certainly beautiful," the woman said as she snapped a photo that took in the house as well as Regina and Dell. Then she waved and the group moved away.

When they had gone, Dell studied her. Her cheeks grew pinker. "I'll bet you were a pistol when you were a kid. Probably gave your teachers a run for their money."

Regina groaned. "I did tell a white lie or two."

He grinned.

"But only in emergencies," she said. "I would never lie about anything important. And I wouldn't have lied now except I was worried. You're an O'Ryan. I'm working very hard on this pictorial. You're making a big move into an unknown market. You don't need bad publicity or to have your picture in the tabloids, especially not with the notation that you were making out in a car in broad daylight."

He tilted his head and couldn't stop smiling. "It might improve my snooty reputation."

"You're not snooty. You're reserved and refined."

"And as Donald the gardener I bet I'm good at pulling weeds, too," he reminded her.

"Agh!" she groaned. "Don't remind me. I don't know what came over me. I just…you were talking about what it takes to be a good O'Ryan. I'm sure that dignity is a part of the O'Ryan credo. I just didn't want anyone to think I had brought you down to the level of a common…man. If we were going to make out, we could at least have had the good taste to do it in the limo."

Dell wanted to smile. She was so cute in her distress. But she *did* sound distressed, and he knew she felt somehow responsible for what had happened. Heaven knew why. He had barely been able to keep his hands off her all day and this wasn't the first time he had kissed her. If anyone was responsible for that hot, sizzling kiss, it was him. And he wasn't ashamed. Right now he wanted nothing more than to taste those lips again. The limo would do. So would any available space where he could hold her, slide his hands over her skin, peel back her clothing and find the treasure that lay beneath. White-hot desire raged through him, but somehow he managed to ignore it. Instead he reached out and gently cupped his palms around her waist.

"Regina, hush," he said, pulling her into his arms. "Don't look like that. You're my wife, and what you and I do together is nobody's business but our own. Kissing my wife is not a crime." Although he knew how ill-advised it was given the tentative nature of their relationship.

But Regina was still staring up at him, uncertainty in her eyes. He couldn't blame her. Things were unsettled and she had already been hurt by a seemingly settled relationship. She was worried. He couldn't have that.

"I told them you were a gardener," she murmured as she leaned against him, her lips moving softly against his chest and driving him mad.

"I know. Do you think I'm a good gardener?" he mused, trying to tease her into a happier mood.

His plan worked. She ducked her head, then leaned back in his arms and looked up, giving him a sheepish smile. "I'm sure you're…at least adequate. But Dell?"

"What?"

"You're a really great kisser." Then she pulled away and hurried into the house.

Dell's eyes widened as he watched her disappear. He couldn't help chuckling. His wife had had the last word in the teasing game. And now he wanted her even more.

CHAPTER ELEVEN

DELL stared at the appointment sheet Louella had given him as if he had never seen an appointment sheet. He was obviously not himself today. And no wonder. All his thoughts were starting to focus on Regina.

Some people might say that was a good thing. A husband should be attentive to his wife. But that wasn't the problem. This wasn't about attentiveness. This was about the fact that she was becoming the driving force in his day. And he very much doubted that she felt the same way.

Especially now that she had confessed that she hadn't really loved Lee but had thought of him as a needy puppy.

Something unpleasant slipped through Dell. He remembered how diligently Regina had been working on this pictorial to promote him to the Chicago prospects, he remembered her work with Edna, her charitable acts with the animal shelter.

He had the very bad feeling that he, Dell O'Ryan, a man who was a mover and a shaker and a powerhouse among the upper echelons of Boston society and Boston businessmen, had become one of his wife's charitable projects. Why else did she keep talking about becoming his friend?

And she didn't want his jewels, Dell reminded himself, remembering their discussion of the Bride Emeralds. Swearing beneath his breath, he stared down at the list of things he had to do, people he had to see. He didn't want to see any of them. He wanted to be with Regina. Too darn much.

The fact that she had admitted enjoying his kiss didn't make it any easier, because now he knew that he could force the issue and she would probably play along.

He didn't want her playing along or taking care of him, but keeping himself from taking things to the next complicated level was becoming more difficult. He needed a good distraction.

Picking up the phone, he made a few calls. Then, with a growl, he picked up the list Louella had given him. Work had always distracted him from his troubles in the past.

Anticipation grew in Regina the closer she got to the door of the mansion. And it was a good anticipation, the kind that left her breathless and aching and...

Stop it, she told herself leaning against the door. The day had been mostly awful. Despite a good early beginning with a shy, glowing bride, it had gone downhill after that with the Vandivers changing half their plans and making more demands, forcing the Belles to redo work and rearrange schedules. Then, while Belle and Julie had been trying to manage the rescheduling, Charlie Wiley had called again, flustering Belle and forcing Julie to tell him Belle was unavailable.

Only one good thing had happened after that and it

had to do with Dell, Regina was sure. Almost against her will, her heart flipped, and the bad day seemed to fade away. That man…

No, not that man. Dell, who was starting to mean too much to her. Just the sound of his name had started to conjure up unwelcome images, desires. That kiss the other day…

Regina shivered in response. She was starting to feel things for her husband, to want to be with him. Which was so wrong. Longing had never been a part of the plan. This whole arrangement was supposed to have been practical. Dell would have a wife and he wouldn't have to worry about the whispers and the media circus of an O'Ryan going through a divorce. She would have a secure and calm existence.

Companionship was allowed. Desire of a sort was to be expected. If they stayed together it would be a real marriage with nothing too far out of the ordinary, but…what was going on inside her wasn't ordinary at all. When Dell had kissed her, she had quite simply lost herself. All that had mattered had been touching Dell, feeling his lips caress hers.

Panic gathered in Regina's stomach. If she continued this way, she was going to get hurt.

"I won't let that happen," she whispered. Somehow, she would have to find a way to protect herself. Still, Dell needed to be thanked for the news she had gotten today.

She climbed the stairs to his office. He wasn't there. That was odd. Dell was almost always home by now. But then for the past two days he'd been spending an amazing amount of time working. The Chicago project, she assumed. Of course. With things heating up after his last trip, he would be too busy to do much else.

A tiny sliver of longing shot through her. *Irrelevant,* she thought. And then Dell appeared in the hallway behind her. He looked tired. His tie was slightly askew, his hair looked as if he had run his fingers through it. He was delightfully rumpled and sexy and far too compelling in spite of it all.

Her first thought was to get closer to him. "Long day?" she asked instead.

His amber eyes turned dark. "Standard," he said, but he had a look in his eyes that told her he would like to come closer, too. But he didn't.

"I had a call from Jaz Ezland who runs the shelter. Phoebe has a new home, a very nice one," she offered. "So do a lot of the dogs we saw the other day. An unusual number of them."

To his credit, he didn't blink. "I'm glad." His voice was warm.

"Dell?"

He waited.

"Thank you. This means so much to me," she said, taking a step closer, her hand outstretched.

In two long strides, Dell was across his room. He dropped one hard, quick kiss on her lips, hesitated, then kissed her again. Longer, deeper.

Her mind sizzled. She rose on her toes. A moan escaped hers.

Immediately Dell froze. "I'm trying very hard to keep from touching you," he said. "Until you're ready for more."

Her immediate thought was that she *was* ready for more. She wanted it all, but she'd spent a lifetime following impulses and this time, a wrong impulse could leave her irreparably damaged. What if things didn't work out? What if he left her? Didn't people always leave?

Dell, took a deep breath. He brushed his fingers lightly

across her cheek, then turned. "Work," he said, and the word sounded more like an order than an explanation.

Within five minutes she heard his office door close. He didn't come out before she went to bed.

Regina lay on her bed that night, wondering what on earth she was doing. That kiss…every kiss they'd shared…

Oh, my word. Dell's lips, his hands…no wonder women wanted her husband so badly. And no wonder Elise Allenby was so heartbroken. Had he kissed *her* that way?

Regina covered her face with her hands. That was none of her business. It was before her time, and it was with a woman…

A woman he had chosen.

Abruptly Regina sat up.

What am I doing? It was true that she'd had doubts earlier about her relationship with Dell, but she had offered him a divorce and he had turned her down. He was the one who had suggested the trial marriage and he was fulfilling his bargain. Hadn't he been doing all that he could to get to know her, even going so far as to go to the shelter with her that day? And he had tried to help her at the ball by extending her business connections.

If things had stalled just because there was a little heat flaring between them, the kind that was bound to appear between any man and woman who had shared living space, surely she could get past that. She hadn't taken a single picture of Dell in days or finished the chapter on him, and time was running out.

You've never been a shy little weakling, Regina, she told herself. *Don't start now.* In the end, this union might not work, but it wasn't going to be because she hadn't done her share. Dell might have money and position and a body that made her shiver. He might be the world's greatest kisser, but she had some skills, too. And tomorrow she was going to get back on the horse...er, back behind the camera and do her part.

Just don't start thinking all this togetherness and touching means more than it does, she reminded herself.

Because despite the heat that flared between them he had already told her multiple times that this would never be a marriage based on love. And if a woman kept that in mind and just did the smart thing, surely she would be okay. Wouldn't she?

Doubts assailed her. *Time to squelch those and take a stand,* she thought, picking up the cell phone lying by her bed. She punched in a number.

"Dell O'Ryan," came over the phone, his voice deep and low and husky. Had he been sleeping already?

"Dell, it's Regina."

A pause followed. "Where *are* you?"

"In bed," she said automatically.

She heard his swift intake of breath. "All right, forget I asked that. Is there an emergency?"

"Not exactly."

"You're calling me from within the house. You could have come to see me."

No, she was brave but not brave enough to go to his room while her emotions were still racketing around inside her body like explosive ping-pong balls.

"Tomorrow, I'm going to finish the photos," she told him. "All right?"

Again, a hesitation. "I'll be ready," he finally said.

For some reason, getting that settled didn't make it any easier to sleep.

* * *

Dell was lifting weights in a private training room in the gym and Regina was taking photos when a news crew from a local cable television station showed up. Apparently his recent excursions with Regina and the fact that she had been following him all week with a camera had come to the attention of a local station that was low on news for the day. Before either of them was aware what was happening the cameras were turned on him and Regina.

"Mrs. O'Ryan, can you tell us how exactly you met your husband?"

Regina's eyes opened wide. Clearly startled and uncomfortable, she hesitated.

Dell frowned. He was just about to tell the man to get lost when Regina shook her head. "We were neighbors. I've known who he was most of my life." Which left a lot out but satisfied the reporter. Dell was proud of his wife for fielding that one so deftly.

"And is it true that Mr. O'Ryan has taken up one of your favorite causes? I understand that a number of pets at a local shelter have suddenly found homes in elite neighborhoods." The man shoved an eight-by-ten of a cute little dachshund into Regina's hands. The dog had melt-your-heart soulful eyes and suddenly Regina looked up at him, wearing a soft, grateful look that would have been a threat to the most icy of men's hearts.

"Trixie. I didn't know she was one of the ones chosen, Dell. And she had that lame leg, too." Regina looked up at him as if he had given her a priceless gift.

He took a step toward her. She took a step toward him, too, but then she seemed to catch herself. She gave him a quick shake of her head. Ah yes, they weren't alone.

"My husband is a very fine man," she said. She looked

up at Dell, and the cameraman turned the lights and camera on the two of them. Regina blinked from the glare.

"I—" she continued, but caught in the whir of the video camera, she looked suddenly self-conscious. "I know this sounds strange coming from a photographer, but I don't wish to be interviewed on film. I'm not—I don't think—" She looked down at her favorite ripped jeans and loose white blouse. She'd been down on the floor only moments earlier taking photos at knee level, and her hair was mussed, strands of the silken stuff kissing her cheeks and temples. She looked a bit wanton, and Dell had a sudden urge to step in front of her and shield her from the view of the other two men.

Instantly he turned to the crew, adopting the icy hauteur he'd learned from a master at the game, his father. "I don't recall okaying this interview."

"You're a public figure, Mr. O'Ryan."

"But this is a private club."

"Yes, but—"

"There are rules, and they're enforced." He had no idea if such rules even existed, although there were people milling about outside this door who probably did know. He didn't bother asking. These two men were not seasoned reporters, and they probably didn't know protocol here, either. From the uncomfortable look the two men gave each other, neither of them wanted to risk a visit from management or the local authorities. Good, they were on the verge of deciding to leave.

But then…

"Excuse me, but I'm in the middle of doing a major photo shoot of my husband. Your cameras are wreaking havoc with the lighting." Regina had apparently found her voice and her resolve. She stood as tall as Dell had ever seen her and faced the men. "If you don't mind, I'd like to finish my work."

Her brown eyes were flecked with gold, he realized, and when she was miffed, they appeared to flash. Her normally creamy complexion turned a dusky rose. Her chest rose and fell with every deep, irritated breath.

With her tousled hair and her fervor, she was mesmerizing. Dell didn't know whether to applaud or to groan. The men turned their attention from him. They forgot about his implied threat.

"We apologize for the lighting, but this is for television," one man argued. "Don't worry, Mrs. O'Ryan, we'll get out of your way soon, and we'll do your husband justice. We'll send you some really nice pictures. Professional quality."

Regina froze. She looked down, her hair covering her face, and when she raised her head again that pretty little chin had come up, she drew her shoulders back and turned her full attention to the intruders. They were twice her size, taller, broader and beefy where she was delicate, but she placed one hand on her denim-clad hip and stared them down as the gist of the man's words settled in.

"If you're trying to imply that I'm merely playing at being a professional or that your credentials and expertise outweigh mine, then you're wrong. In fact—" Regina whirled to turn her Hasselblad on the camera crew "—it occurs to me that the pictorial of my husband should engage *all* aspects of his life, including the media's attraction to him. Would you mind moving a little closer and looking as if you're having a conversation with Dell? Yes, both of you." She didn't wait for a response. She just started snapping shots.

"What? Whoa, wait a minute," the clearly startled

men objected, but Regina kept shooting pictures. "Tilt your head slightly," she ordered. "Yes, you know the routine and the importance of setting and contrast and mood. Try to catch that beam of light filtering in through that skylight. Ask my husband a question. Any question. The answer doesn't matter, only the realism of you looking as if you're actually talking to him. Oh, yeah, that's it exactly. I love this!"

Her camera clicked off shot after shot. Although she had started off insulted, Dell could tell that she soon forgot her pique. She was thoroughly enjoying herself, losing herself in the moment. And in almost no time the men began to join in, infected by her enthusiasm and technique, suggesting shots. By the time she was done, they were both looking at her as if they'd been given a rare gift. They'd obviously never met anyone quite like Regina, and when she finally lowered her camera and sighed with satisfaction, they were half in love with her, Dell thought. And who could blame them?

"Mr. O'Ryan, your wife's something else. She flipped that camera like a juggler at the circus, but we can't go back to work with absolutely nothing to show. Come on, give us a break. How about a couple of answers and a newsworthy moment here?" one of them coaxed. "We'll make it good."

And, Dell thought, they were sure to mention that his wife was a very talented woman. After the last few minutes, he had no doubt that they would paint her in a highly flattering light. All of that would be a definite boon to Regina and the Belles. What was a man to do?

Give in, Dell thought. Promote and protect his wife. No question.

"All right, here's a bit of truth, gentlemen," Dell

said. "My wife, Regina, grew up not far from me, almost beneath my nose, in fact, but I never knew she existed until recently. I must have been blind, because anyone can see that she's both talented and lovely and that I am an incredibly lucky man to have found such a treasure." And with that, he stepped closer to Regina, tilted her face up and dropped a kiss on her lips. Her eyes drifted shut and he tasted her sweetness. She rose ever so slightly on her toes. Her palms pressed against his chest. Then she curled her fingers into his T-shirt and pulled just a touch closer, returning his kiss.

Dell's world began to tilt. He slipped a hand beneath the silk of her hair as he deepened the kiss.

"Oh, yeah," the cameraman said. "That's perfect."

As if he had shot her, Regina's eyes flew open. Warm color drifted up her cheeks and she leaned back. Instantly Dell released her.

"That's off the record," she stammered to the men.

One of them saluted her as they gathered their equipment. "I can't wait to see those pictures, Mrs. O'Ryan. Will you e-mail a couple to the station?"

Then they were out the door. Dell was left standing there with his wife's hands still bunched in his shirt. And then in the next minute she had backed away and turned all business. "I really have to get to the shop. And I have to see what I can do with these pictures. This rounds things out nicely. I think we're almost through," she said.

Dell nearly swore. He had embarrassed her publicly, and she was going into hiding. He could tell. Which couldn't mean anything good. The look in her eyes was unhappy, and there had been too much unhappiness in her life this year. His plan to make this marriage of convenience truly convenient for him might not work for her, he finally acknowledged. She had had a terrible year. She had lost so much. A child.

And if the child had been born they wouldn't be considering whether to stay together or not. Their daughter would have bound them.

The thought slipped in, but Dell discarded it. A child should never be given the burden of maintaining his parents' marriage. It didn't work that way, as he well knew. If a couple was going to stay together, that should be a choice built on reason. Not on necessity, not on love and certainly not on the mere flash and fire of passion.

But he didn't say any of that. It brought the tentative nature of his relationship with Regina under the microscope and he wasn't ready to examine it right now.

"I should have sent them away," he said.

She shook her head. "No, it made sense. We're trying to be a couple. That means appearing as a couple, united, normal, even touching at times.

"But...I don't think I'm very good at this, Dell. As you know, I tend to be impetuous, but I can't be impetuous now. I can't afford any more drastic mistakes, especially not when I've made so many already." She looked up at him, uncertain.

"Regina, I didn't mean to upset you."

"No, it's not you. It's me. I..." She leaned closer as if to tell him something, then blanched and quickly whirled away. "I'm sorry, but I really have to go to work. I'll see you later."

And without another word, she hurried out the door.

Dell was left there standing in the silent and suddenly

empty room. He felt like kicking himself. What had he said or done?

A lot, and obviously one or all of those things had spooked Regina and pushed her farther away. Once again he had handled things all wrong with his wife and now she was on the run.

A desperate need to get things back on a comfortable level took hold of him, and that in itself was alarming. He didn't want to feel so much or so strongly about a woman.

So what was he going to do about that? This sweet, impetuous woman was feeling as if she had to put reins on herself in order to make this trial marriage work.

That was something to think about…

CHAPTER TWELVE

"YOU'RE looking pale, Regina," Serena said. "Is everything all right?"

"I'm just a bit tired." Which was as close to the truth as Regina could get. She was also scared. Positively petrified in fact. This trial marriage had seemed so simple at first, and now...she didn't want to think about the now or what had been happening to her heart lately.

Serena looked concerned. "It's not your husband, is it?" she asked.

Regina wondered how Serena could always see right through to her fears, but she shook her head. "Dell is great," she answered, and it was the truth. That in itself was alarming. She didn't want to start thinking of him in superlatives or begin to feel emotions that could never be returned. What was she going to do? How was she going to get past this?

Her thoughts were interrupted by a bell jangling over the door.

Belle smiled at the man who entered. Probably a salesman, but Belle knew how to handle salesmen so that they left without feeling they had been kicked out.

"May I help you?" she asked the man who appeared to be in his mid-fifties with salt and pepper hair.

"I sure hope so," the man said. "I'm hoping to find Belle Mackenzie. I was here once before but missed her. Would you happen to know where I might find her?"

Immediately Belle looked wary. Regina's attention went on full-alert.

"I'm Belle. You're Rae Anne's friend, aren't you?" Belle asked. Her tone seemed a bit chilly.

"Yes, ma'am, I am. And so are you, I understand." There was a tone in the man's voice that snagged Regina's attention. The man was looking at Belle as if she were the last piece of chocolate cake on the plate.

"Yes, Rae Anne and I go way back. She thinks she knows me." Her tone indicated that Belle disagreed and that she was not happy that her friend had sent this man around.

The man, however, grinned broadly. "So, you don't want to sell your car?"

Belle blinked. "My car? The Rolls?"

"I hear she's a real beauty. A vintage model and the prettiest shade of forest-green a man has ever seen."

Instantly Belle looked even more flustered. "Oh, yes, Rae Anne said you were interested in my car."

For the first time all day Regina wanted to smile, too. Belle had been very upset that Rae Anne had been trying to set her up with this man, but now maybe that wasn't true? Regina wondered how any woman could understand anything that went on in a man's head. No wonder women got hurt so often.

"I'm Charlie Wiley," the man was telling Belle. "And yes, I'm very interested. I hear you've got a 1930 Rolls-

Royce Phantom II. I've been looking for one like that. Could I see it?"

Unfortunately the bell clanged again and a customer came through the door looking for Callie. With Julie on her lunch break, Belle took over the task of meeting and greeting and getting the woman back to where she needed to be.

Regina gave Charlie a smile and went back to her task of changing the photos she had hanging on the wall. Serena worked on the dress on the display mannequin. By the time Belle finished and turned back, the customer had been tended to and Charlie was studying Belle as if she were some strange sort of wonderful exotic creature he had never encountered before.

"About the car," Belle was saying.

"The car? Oh…yes, the Rolls Phantom II is sure a beauty." But he was looking at Belle as if she were the beauty.

And Belle was looking a bit flustered. Regina could relate.

"I'm sorry. I can't do this," Belle said suddenly.

"You don't want to sell your car," he said sadly.

"It was my late husband's."

Regina raised a brow. Belle's words made it sound as if Belle had undergone a recent loss, but Matthew had been gone many years.

Now, Charlie was looking sad and concerned. He looked as if he was going to go over to Belle and hug her. He even took a step forward. "I understand. I lost my wife. It's difficult to give up the things they loved. It's just that when I talked to Rae Anne she seemed to indicate that you might be interested."

"Interested?"

"In selling the car. I really want that car." But he was looking at Belle's lips.

She licked them. "I'm afraid I can't do that. Not yet."

"All right then," Charlie said. "Thank you for talking to me, at least. But, if you change your mind, let me know." Then he walked out of the shop.

When Charlie was gone, Belle seemed to deflate. She started fanning herself. She looked at Regina and Serena with a frown. "If you tell anyone I made a fool of myself, I will flatly deny it."

A tiny sympathetic smile lifted Regina's lips. "You were just fine, Belle. But…you know it wasn't the car. He liked *you*."

"Chicken feathers. He's younger than me, he's thinner than me and I am going to have Rae Anne's head on a platter. With gravy. I actually thought for a while that she was trying to fix me up with the man. But he was only after my car. You don't think he saw what I was thinking, do you?"

But she didn't wait for an answer. Belle walked away fanning herself. "I have got to go call Rae Anne and give her a piece of my mind before the next wedding party comes in."

Regina and Serena exchanged a look. "It's never easy with men, is it?" Serena asked.

Regina didn't answer, but she totally agreed. It was her last coherent thought of the day. Customers began to swarm. One of the senior Vandivers called with even more changes. Regina, who took the call, could hear Liz Vandiver screaming at someone in the background.

"Just let me get through a few more weeks," she told herself. "Let everything turn out all right." But she knew that it wasn't the Vandivers she was thinking about.

* * *

Dell hesitated outside his wife's door. It was early, but then early was a necessity. If he didn't catch her now, she would be gone for work. Raising his hand, he rapped on the solid mahogany, then waited and rapped again.

Ten seconds later, the door opened. He looked down at Regina. She was wearing a cropped, red v-necked T-shirt.

His mind began to short-circuit but he stopped himself. That was not what this was about. Instead he looked down at her feet.

"You have kittens on your feet," he said.

Immediately she looked down, too. "Oh, yes. Dell?"

"I know. What am I doing here? What do I want?"

What he wanted was to kiss her. "I'm taking you out for a day on the town," he said.

Those caramel eyes opened wide. "I have work."

"I know. Me, too. But…"

She waited. "Yesterday," he explained. "And all the days that have passed…I think we're losing sight of something important. We were once friends of a sort. We should try for that again. At least one day to be sure."

Of whether we're going to make it or not, he added to himself.

Suddenly she smiled. "You're kidding, right? Take a whole day off when it wasn't in your appointment book? I'll bet you've never played hooky once in all your life. You can't make me believe that Louella would have approved."

"Louella would be appropriately horrified." His parents, too.

Regina patted his arm. "Then it's good that you have me, a woman with some experience in these matters. I'll call in sick for you."

"Excuse me?"

"You know, like when you're in high school and you

want to go to the beach but you need a parental excuse, you have to get an adult, or at least someone who sounds like an adult to call in sick at the school."

"You did that?" He chuckled.

"Once or twice when I was younger. Nowadays, hardly ever. I'm good at my job, I'm needed and I enjoy it. But after yesterday when the Vandivers were acting up, I could use a few hours of freedom. Today was supposed to be a prep day, not a photo day, so I can swing some time off. Tomorrow I'm booked, so if I'm going to play it has to be now."

And what man could turn away from that?

"I'll leave you to get ready," he said.

"Where are we going?"

Dell blinked. "I have no idea."

Her laugh caught him square in the gut. "I'll bet that's another first for you. No plan. Leave it to me. I know the perfect places for friends to hang out together. You don't have to worry about a thing."

Except for keeping this platonic, he reminded himself.

Regina couldn't stop smiling. She had dragged Dell all over the place today. They had visited a park where she'd fed him popcorn and cherry slushes and asked him to push her on the swings and then had offered to push him because she was pretty sure that he hadn't had a lot of opportunity to spend time on swings. Playgrounds probably hadn't been approved recreational activities by his parents. They'd walked part of The Freedom Trail and taken a side trip in order to walk through the Mapparium, the three-story stained-glass globe at The Mary Baker Eddy Library. She had even taken him on the MBTA blue line down to the waterfront and he hadn't complained a bit about the pace or the way she was charging ahead and leading him around. Dell had lived in Boston all his life but he had never ridden the subway. O'Ryans didn't. That hadn't been a surprise. What *had* surprised her was that he had never taken the ferry over to the Boston Harbor Islands.

Now they were on Georges Island having a picnic. "You haven't taken many pictures today," he noted.

She laughed. "Yes, it's hard to believe, isn't it? Most people who know me think me and my camera are joined at the hip."

"You're not?" he teased.

"Okay, most of the time I am. Taking photos is almost like talking, to me. It's a form of communication, but today wasn't for taking lots of pictures. It was for fun."

"It *has* been fun. Still I wish you'd show me more of your work. I've seen some of your shots, of course, the ones on the shop walls and the few you have at home, but you don't have many at home."

She shrugged. "It didn't feel right, but I'll show you the ones I've taken of you."

"That's work, though."

Regina crossed her arms. "It was not work. I did that out of…"

Love. The word just floated right in there. "Marital responsibility," she said. What a dry-sounding phrase.

Dell didn't look as if he liked it, either.

"Maybe friendship, too," she said, using the word she was beginning to hate. This day had been fun and wonderful, but there was just something about her husband that didn't make her feel friendly. She felt more.

Ugh, was she pathetic or what? The man had practically offered her the world; a marriage, a mansion, his name and protection, his friendship, even passion. To ask for more would be so wrong. Not to mention impossible, since it wasn't at all what he wanted.

Don't think about that. Don't think about that, she ordered herself. *Don't mess up the day.*

"So…friend and trial husband," she said, trying to keep her tone light, "you're Mr. Competitive, aren't you?"

"Hmm, that sounds like a trick question, but I'll bite," he said with a smile that practically stole every breath in her body. "Yes, friend and trial wife. My Mrs. O'Ryan," he added, and it was almost all Regina could do to keep from launching herself into his arms. "I've been told that I'm competitive."

"Good. You'll need your competitive spirit for the next half hour. Otherwise, I'm going to beat the pants off of you at Frisbee." She stood and pulled an orange disk out of the bag she had brought with her.

Flopping onto his back in the grass, Dell groaned. "I just ate and you want me to run and jump?"

"And catch," she agreed, placing a hand on her hip. "You grew up in that great big house with all those rules and expectations. I'll bet you never even played this before."

"I'm an O'Ryan, not an alien from another planet." He rose and moved out and away from her.

"Hmm, that might be close to the same thing." She tossed the disk his way.

He lunged, catching it with ease, then twisted and whipped it back her way.

"Very nice, Mr. O'Ryan."

"My father didn't take us on family outings or feel that common playgrounds were classy enough, but he felt it was important for O'Ryan males to have some athletic skill. There were goals to be met. Achievement was stressed."

"Achievement is great, but it's not fun." She flipped the disk high so that it looped back toward him lazily.

"Fun is overrated, young lady. The most common person can have fun, but an O'Ryan sets the bar for achievement and success," Dell said with such an imperious tone that Regina could almost hear his father lecturing a young and still wide-eyed Dell. It was no wonder her husband spent so much time working and so little time playing.

"Your father said that?"

Dell didn't question her assumption that the quote had been his father's. "Don't worry. I survived childhood, Regina," he said. "And I grew up to marry a woman who knows the value of cherry slushes and playgrounds and play," he said. "And who was willing to spend a day teaching me all the things she thought I needed to know."

He released the disk, sending it her way. Unfortunately Regina was so choked up by Dell's heartfelt assessment of her that she failed to reach out quickly enough. She leaned too far the wrong way and the disk nearly hit her in the head, leading her to duck backward and fall right onto her back. She lay there, dazed.

Dell came running up. "Regina, are you all right?" He leaned over her, his amber eyes worried.

Her head was still spinning and with the sun behind him, her husband was so dazzlingly gorgeous. No wonder Elise Allenby wanted him.

"Regina?" Dell held up three fingers. "How many?" She giggled. "I'm fine."

"How many?" he ordered.

"You're pretty good at all this lord and commander

stuff," she said. But Dell looked ready to explode. "Three," she said primly. "And thank you."

"Good," he said in reference to her finger counting. "And thank you for what?"

"I don't know. For suggesting this day and for going along with my version of what you had planned. I know all of this—" she held out her hands "—is outside your comfort zone. And it was nice of you to agree to take the subway instead of bringing the limo."

His smile was mischievous. "Yes, it was a terrible sacrifice. We O'Ryans have to have our comfort or we throw tantrums."

"You know what I mean." She sat up and hit him lightly on the arm.

"I do. And…this is nice."

"I can't believe you haven't been here before. There's so much history in these islands. I mean, the only manned lighthouse remaining in the States is on the island, and here on Georges Island there's supposed to be a ghost. Prisoners from the Confederate Army were kept here and the legendary Lady in Black was a prisoner's wife. Thirty-four islands right outside your home and no one ever took you here. That's so…"

He smiled.

She frowned. "What?"

"You don't have to be indignant for me, Regina. I'm not a poor-little-rich-boy anymore. I'm a man and I don't have to conform to the rules. I can do whatever I like."

She looked up at him to see if he was telling the truth or just trying to make her feel better, but kneeling beside her, he was so close…so warm, so Dell…

He leaned down and kissed her. Slowly. Thoroughly. She surged up, grasping his biceps to keep from falling backward, but there was no need. Dell had wrapped one strong arm around her. He was holding her close. *I can't let myself fall any further than I already have* was her last coherent thought as she lifted her face and returned his kiss. His lips were warm, his touch was magic; the air around them sizzled.

Dell kissed her again, more deeply.

"Look, Mommy, those people are kissing," she heard a child's voice say.

Immediately Regina sat up and pushed away. She stared at her husband with regret and desire and a hefty portion of guilt. So much for not being able to fall. All she had to do was get too close to Dell and she did all kinds of stupid things.

"Well, that was very nice," she said primly. "A nice way to top off the day." She tried to rise.

"Regina." Dell's voice was stern. "I—"

"If you say you're sorry or try to take some sort of responsibility, I will hit you very hard. This was supposed to be a day of play and a day of no regrets, and we were playing…sort of, so don't regret. At least there were no camera crews this time. No harm done."

He studied her for a moment silently, but then he moved aside, rose and helped her to her feet. When she dared to look up at him again, he was wearing a speculative look.

"What?" she demanded.

"You taste like cherry slushes," he said.

"Well, that's good then. I like cherry slushes."

"And so do I. A lot more than I want to."

Which was a totally depressing thought, since it was obvious they weren't talking about cherry slushes at all. He wanted her but he didn't like it one bit. It didn't fit in with his plan for this marriage. But when they got back to the house and she turned her phone back on and picked up her messages, all thoughts of plans fled.

She turned to Dell and she knew that her face was ghostly white. "The Vandivers have canceled. We're out money, but worse, they were going to be our ticket to success and lots more business. Instead once word gets out that they've canceled our contract, the lemmings will start to flee."

All that work, all her friends, all their dreams…

"Regina," Dell said gently. "Come here."

That was all it took, that deep voice laden with complete sympathy. Without another word, Regina threw herself into her husband's arms.

CHAPTER THIRTEEN

DELL caught Regina and pulled her close. "I'm so sorry, Regina, but please...don't worry. I can help you."

"No."

"The Vandivers are asses, and they shouldn't be allowed to harm you this way just because they're selfish. You know I have the means. I won't even feel the dent, and—"

Immediately she pulled back. "No," she said again. "No, please. I appreciate your offer so much, Dell, and I know you don't understand, but I can't take your help. All my life, I've struggled to prove that I'm good enough, that I can do things, that I'm not a screw-up, and if I take money from you for this, then I haven't done anything."

He opened his mouth to object but she shook her head. "Don't mouth the usual platitudes. I know what I am and what I'm not. Believe me, I know my strengths, but this business with the Vandivers...it hurts the people I care about. I'm so angry and disappointed, I can barely think straight. I just need time and I need...I don't know, but I know I can't take your money to fix things. Through thick and thin, disappointments and trials and years of work and friendship, the Belles have come together on this and it's ours, mistakes and all. I can't inject you into this. I can't become indebted to you. If you and I end... feeling that I owed you money...if we end our marriage, it has to be clean."

Her words lashed through him. "And if we don't?"

She hesitated. "That has to be clean, too. Nothing messy. No complications."

But what Dell saw in her eyes, that hesitation, told him that she was thinking of ending things. She needed to be able to walk away totally free. Something dark and hot and wrong ripped at him, but he fought to contain it. She was hurting right now. Scared. And she wouldn't let him help her. What could he do?

Nothing. Apparently absolutely nothing. So, he pulled her closer into his arms and just held on. That was all he could give her, all she would allow. His strength. His comfort.

When it grew dark and she was still wide-eyed and in pain, he carried her to bed and lay her down.

"Don't leave me," she whispered. "Stay. I don't want to be alone with my thoughts."

He nodded and lay down next to her, pulling her body up against his as he rested his chin on the top of her silky hair and stroked one hand down her back. "Do you want to tell me your thoughts? You don't have to."

"I know." And she didn't say anything for long minutes. He listened to her breathing, felt her shudder when he shifted her to pull her closer still.

"My parents wanted me to be an accountant," she finally said. "Something practical. They were so disappointed when I insisted on becoming a photographer. It was there in every look, every word. They had only one child, one shot. They had hoped for someone they could brag about to their friends, not someone who at times ended up praying that the jar of peanut butter would hold out until she sold something."

Her words echoed through his body, a soft whisper. "Didn't they ever see your work and how good it is?"

She pulled back in his arms and a hint of a painful smile flickered across her face. "Well, they did try to smile politely when they realized that they weren't going to be able to change me, but to them it was just irresponsible to try to sell people pictures. I was just playing at being an adult in their eyes. And now they're gone, swept away in a boating accident before I had a chance to make them proud just once."

"Maybe now they understand," he whispered. "Maybe wisdom and true appreciation comes with dying and they're looking down seeing what they hadn't seen before."

Even in the dark he could see that she didn't believe him. "You obviously never met my parents."

"I've met you, and you really are incredibly talented."

Regina leaned forward. He felt her small smile against his chest. Her muffled thank you warmed his skin. Against his will, desire shunted through him. He started to turn away slightly.

But in the dark she caught at him. "No. It was inevitable that we would do this, finally. I've wanted it before and I want it more now. Tonight, I need to touch you and have you touch me. I am, after all, the woman who lives for today. Can't be an artist without that attitude. Maybe tomorrow will never come or it won't be the tomorrow you want, so take today. I think maybe

I forgot that in the past year. Today is important. Maybe it's more important than yesterday or tomorrow."

With that, she pulled herself up and slid her arms around his neck. She kissed him and gave him what he'd been dying to have.

Dell gave up the battle he'd been fighting for too long. He swept his wife beneath him. He kissed her the way he'd been wanting to for weeks, tasting her, savoring her, plunging his fingers into her hair.

She rose to meet him, tearing at the buttons on his shirt, a participant, not a mere recipient. Together they undressed him.

"You're beautiful," she said. "You've always been so beautiful."

"I think those are my lines," he said, reaching for her.

"No. They're not. They're definitely mine."

"I'll show you," he argued. With only the rising moon for light, he found Regina, slipped her out of her pretty little shoes, her blouse and jeans. He removed the tiny, pale blue scraps that remained, shielding her from him.

For half a second, with moonlight in her eyes, he saw the self-doubt in her expression.

"You're incredibly lovely," he said fiercely. "And you're driving me mad with the need to touch. So, my pretty little wife, if you're going to change your mind, then—"

"And miss this? That's so not going to happen," she said, cutting him off and giving him a beautiful smile. "I'll even agree to let you tell me that I'm lovely if you'll touch me, Dell. Right now. Please."

"You can't know how much of a pleasure it will be." He traced his fingers over her sensitive lips. He kissed her eyes, her cheeks, her throat. Then together he and his wife found each other in the dark. He lost his legendary self-control. She enchanted him more than any princess could. They touched in ways they had never touched before.

And when he entered her, he knew it had to be right. It had to be special for her, because she was special.

It was. He loved her into the night, reveling in her softness and breathing in the scent of her hair. His fingertips learned the contours of her body. He discovered that what he'd thought of as ecstasy was only a shadow of the real thing. And, when the morning came, and he looked over to see Regina sleeping peacefully, her dark hair against her pale skin, he knew he might never know a night this magical again.

Because the sand was almost out of the hourglass. A decision would be made soon. What if it were the wrong one? She still hadn't told him that she would stay. A silent protest roared through his brain.

The stark light flowed in through the window, illuminating everything. It woke Regina. When she opened her eyes and looked at him, she smiled at first. And then he saw it. Just a hint. The smallest trace.

Regret. Cinderella's magical evening had flown, and unforgiving reality reined once again.

He had just made love to his wife for the first time and it had been earth-shattering. But now it was morning, and she was remorseful.

"Good morning," he said and gave her a reassuring smile she didn't return. "Don't be sorry," he said.

"I'm not. I'm happy."

Had a woman ever sounded less happy? What was he to say to that? "Good, because I don't regret a minute," he said and kissed her softly. Then, sure that she wanted to forget and aware that she had important matters and work she had to tend to, he climbed from bed and went to get dressed and face the day. There was something he absolutely had to do and it wouldn't wait.

Regina came home from work not sure what to expect. The shop had been too silent. Whether that was because the word had already spread that they had lost their biggest account or just the result of an unusually hot day didn't really matter.

"It's probably better that we don't have too much business," Julie had said. "With expressions like ours, anyone who came through the door would most likely run away."

But Regina knew that her own woebegone expression had less to do with the Vandiver cancellation than what had happened last night. What had been a possibility before had turned into a reality. She had lowered her defenses and made love with Dell. It had been wonderful, blissful...devastating.

Because now she had no protection remaining. She was falling in love with her husband when he had specifically told her not to expect love.

Would she never learn?

She was still asking that question when she warily pushed open the door at home later that evening. In an eerily familiar scene, Dell was waiting for her much like that day she had asked him for the divorce.

Regina's heart hurt. It wasn't that she thought he would ask her for a divorce. Rather, it was that she knew he never would. He would be content staying married to her without love.

Could she do that?

"Is something wrong?" she asked.

"Not at all. Everything's going according to plan," he whispered, dropping a light kiss on her lips. But there was a slight tension in his stance. Did he suspect that she felt more than he did? Was it a burden?

"Regina, I have a dinner party tonight at seven. If you're willing, I'd very much like you to come." His manner was so formal, so very Dell as she had known him from afar once, so solicitous of her. What could she say?

"Of course. I'll just get ready."

"Thank you," he said. There was a hint of regret in his eyes, but he gave her a smile as she left. A short time later when they walked out the door, he handed her into the limo.

The drive was quiet, the house they pulled up to imposing but not as imposing as Dell's mansion.

"Regina, I'd like you to meet Mr. and Mrs. Roger Stanson, and this is their daughter Jennifer. This is my wife, Regina," he said as smiles and polite greetings were exchanged. Regina didn't fail to notice the appreciative glance the young woman gave Dell. For half a second, she was tempted to move closer to him, but that would have been juvenile, wouldn't it? And she would never want to embarrass Dell.

"My wife is a talented photographer for The Wedding Belles, a wedding planning service," Dell volunteered as dinner progressed. "She and her colleagues offer only the best."

"Oh, that's so nice to know," Mrs. Stanson said with a smile.

Regina wasn't sure what to say. It certainly wasn't the first time Dell had promoted her, but he'd never mentioned the Belles before. He was obviously trying to be helpful.

He might not believe in love, but he was an incredibly generous person. If only she could settle for that...

Tears gathered in her throat, but she choked them back. Steadfastly she kept her eyes off her husband, afraid her feelings would be too obvious.

"Dell is an incredible catch, my dear. I can't believe a woman ever got him to settle down. He'd been dodging marriage for a long time," Mrs. Stanson said. She obviously meant it as a compliment to Regina, but all Regina could think was that she had entrapped Dell by getting pregnant.

"I'm very lucky," she admitted as Dell's hand covered her own.

"Not as lucky as I am, sweetheart," Dell said, taking her hand and placing his lips against it. Instantly her body was on full-alert. What was going on here? What was Dell doing?

"You two are so romantic," Jennifer said with excitement in her eyes.

"It's probably Regina's work," Dell said. "When a woman and her friends spend all day turning girls into princesses and making magic for brides and grooms, that tends to rub off. My wife knows how to make romance come alive."

A slight bit of tension crept into Regina's soul. What *was* Dell doing? But then she knew. He was selling her.

"Jennifer's getting married soon," Mrs. Stanson said. "As she's our only child, of course we want the very best for her."

What could Regina say? "She should have the very best. Every bride should. Every woman should have that special day when everything that happens is a reflection of the love she and her groom feel for each other." Which was, indeed, what Regina believed. *But I would never have brought it up,* she thought, *without Dell steering the conversation in that direction.*

"I like that," Mrs. Stanson said. "It sounds as if you really care about your clients."

"I do. I really do," Regina told her. Which was of course the truth, and seemed to make Mrs. Stanson positively glow.

The rest of the evening passed in polite conversation, but when they finally left to return home and climbed into the limo, Regina turned to her husband. "Dell...I'm so very grateful for what you're trying to do, but you can't save me every time I fall. It doesn't work that way. I'm not Lee."

"I know that, but I couldn't not do this."

In that instant, she knew that that was the relationship they would have. She would fall more in love with him. He would be kind and gallant and wonderfully passionate. He would make love to her gently, sending her to heaven and beyond and every day she would be more distressingly, hopelessly in love. Sooner or later she might let the words slip out in the night.

He would know, and though it wouldn't be the kind of marriage he wanted he would still never desert her. He would stay. Out of duty and honor and because he wouldn't want to hurt her.

And it won't be him hurting me, she thought as they came to a halt. *It will be me. I'm hurting me. I'm the one in love here. I'm the one who stepped out of line and who didn't obey the rules.* Just like always. Only, unlike her parents, Dell would never reprimand her. He would just never love her.

Her heart was shattering. The truth was damning.

When the car arrived at the mansion, she turned to him. "I'm very tired," she said apologetically, even though she wanted nothing more than to throw herself into his arms and make love.

He stroked her cheek gently. "Get some rest then. Everything will be fine, Regina."

But it wouldn't be. There never had been a chance of it working.

She went upstairs, but she didn't sleep. Instead she dragged out everything she had for the book. She worked through the night filling in the missing pieces that completed the project and presented a true picture of Dell the man, not just Dell the millionaire. When morning came at last, she was done. An electronic package went out to numerous locations with a few clicks on the keyboard.

Carefully she packed, choosing only the things she needed most. Then she went to Dell's study, her bag in hand.

He took one look and rose from his chair. Rounding the desk, he started toward her.

She took a step back and held out a hand.

"Is it because of last night, because you asked me not to help you and I ignored your wishes?" he asked.

"No," she said, shaking her head vehemently. "Courting the Stansons wasn't like handing me money. It was a nice gesture. I just…" She looked up at him and fought back tears. "We just don't suit, Dell. I like you. I've always liked you." Which was so far from what she felt it was just totally inadequate as a description. "But…I can't be happy here."

And that was the complete truth.

"Forgive me," she said. "I never meant to bring

scandal or notoriety to your family, and I'm sure the divorce will at least bring you some negative attention."

The word that fell from Dell's lips was one she'd never heard him use, but he quickly composed himself. He advanced with his hand out.

"You didn't bring scandal," he said. "I wish you could be happy here, but if you can't…"

He took the hand she had held out to meet his and pulled her close, snaking his arm around her. For a few seconds he held on tight and Regina thought he would surely see her heart breaking to bits. Then he pulled back, gave her a quick kiss and said goodbye. He turned back to his desk.

Regret filled her soul. He might say that she had not brought scandal to his life, but she had obviously disrupted his life. He had been on track to a bright future with no shaky spots when she had come along.

At least his future will still be bright eventually, she reassured herself as she left the house for the last time. When the truth became known, when the women of his world discovered that Dell O'Ryan was a free man again, there would be celebrating in the streets.

Eventually there would be another Mrs. O'Ryan, one who fit the mold.

And I—

Regina couldn't finish her thought. Thinking of a world without Dell was too hard to bear. And there was still so much to do before she left him forever.

CHAPTER FOURTEEN

DELL had never been an emotional or demonstrative man. He had lived most of his life completely in control of his emotions, but these past two days...

Had he really thrown a glass against the wall in his office?

He rubbed a hand back through his hair and forced himself to try to concentrate on work and on forgetting. But it wasn't working, and he knew why. He had fallen in love with his wife, and she didn't want to be married to him anymore.

Every impulse in his body screamed at him to go to her and ask her to give him more time, but he knew that wouldn't work. Somehow he had to get through this.

"And I will just as soon as I make sure she's all right," he promised himself.

He picked up the phone and dialed. Within seconds, a voice answered.

"Belle? It's Dell O'Ryan."

Was that a gasp? "You have a lot of nerve calling here."

A thousand questions ran through his brain, but only three mattered. "Why? Where is she? How is she?"

"She's here." Was that Natalie? Had Belle put him on speakerphone?

"As in listening?"

"No. We wouldn't let her talk to you. She's in her studio with a client." That was most definitely Audra.

"But we know you hurt her."

Pain exploded in Dell's brain. He didn't even know who had made the comment. He didn't care. "How do you know she's hurt?"

"She slept at the shop two days in a row and she looks like hell," Belle said. "I don't know what's going on between you two. Even as close as we all are, Regina would never discuss her marriage. She'd feel it was a betrayal of her vows, but…"

"I would feel the same way," Dell said, "but in this case I'm too worried about Regina to keep quiet any longer." He explained what had been going on between him and his wife, her request for a divorce and the agreement that had followed.

"She wants out," he said, not bothering to keep the despair from his voice.

A long silence ensued. "No, she thinks she broke the pact." Serena's voice was unmistakable.

Slowly a tiny thread of hope slipped through Dell. "I don't understand. Explain that."

Someone gave a long sigh. "Regina has never been the type of woman for a practical marriage. It just isn't possible in her world. She's emotion personified. If she decided she couldn't stay, it was because she loves you."

Dell wasn't buying that. "Or because she realized that I love her and she didn't want to hurt me."

Now the silence lengthened. "But which one is it?" Belle asked, her voice less accusatory now. "You'll never know if you just leave things the way they are, will you?"

Doubt assailed Dell. He didn't want to make things

more difficult for Regina by making her listen to his declarations. The thought of her having to spell out the fact that she could never love him was like a thousand knives in his heart, but...

"I'll tell her the truth," he said.

"That could work. Or she might believe you're just humoring her and being gallant. Regina has said more than once that you're a good guy."

Callie was right. Words weren't enough, not for someone as amazing and complex as Regina.

"Thank you," he told them and started to hang up.

"Wait! What are you going to do?" Belle demanded.

"I don't know. Just don't tell her that I called."

Dell hung up the phone, no plan in sight. He waited. He thought. He took a pen and paper, but for the first time in his life, no plan emerged. How did a man try to win a woman who had been hurt by so many people all of whom should have been on her side? What could he do? *And what if she still turns me down?*

Dread seized him. Trying again with Regina was a serious gamble and he had never been a gambler. What if he lost? And what should he do?

He sat there for a long time, uncertain where to turn. The sun began to sink. The sky turned rosy and purple, and as if the heavens had heard his questions, the answer finally dropped in from nowhere. *What would Regina do?* What would his flamboyant, fiery wife do?

The answer was so obvious. *Something big. Something risky and unexpected.* He might have to connive a little, play hooky, tell a few white lies and throw caution and dignity out the window.

In six seconds flat he had Louella on the telephone, firing off instructions.

"She's changed you, I see," Louella said, giving a sniff.

"Yes, she has," he said with a smile.

"And you don't mind that she's practically papered Chicago with stories about how you have been helping former prostitutes?"

Dell raised a brow. "Excuse me?"

Was that a yelp of delight from Louella? "I knew you didn't know about it. I've been keeping tabs on your wife. The word hit the Internet today. She wrote a big article, lots of pictures. Most of it good, she probably thinks, but that picture with the prostitute is all over the image searches. If you don't believe me, look it up yourself."

He did. There he was with Edna. And there he was with Maynard. With the two cameramen. The captions were all glowing. And only one person was missing. Regina herself.

"Your father wouldn't have approved of some of that stuff," Louella said. "And he wouldn't have approved of that picture those two cameramen put on the Internet the other day, either. Your wife looks like a prostitute herself. I think her tongue might have been in your mouth."

"You don't say." Dell did a new search and there he was with Regina, locked in each other's arms. They looked...right together.

"Your father—" Louella began again.

"Is no longer your boss," Dell said. "I am. And actually, my wife is, too. If you have a problem with that, Louella, I'm sure we can make some sort of early retirement arrangement."

She sputtered. "I—"

"I believe the words you're looking for are 'I apologize, Mr. O'Ryan and I will never insult your wife again.'"

Louella muttered the words but Dell knew they would eventually have to work something different out. He didn't care about that now. But there was one thing more.

"Don't bother with those instructions I gave you earlier," he told his secretary. "I've decided that this requires my personal attention."

He hung up the phone, took a deep breath and thought of the woman he adored. Today he was going to risk everything he had ever been and said and done. If he failed, he would look like a hopelessly pathetic chump in the eyes of the world. That kind of attitude could even affect his business. It was almost akin to leaping off a cliff onto the rocks. Not the type of thing an O'Ryan did, ever.

Dell pushed back from his desk…and leaped.

Regina felt as if her feet were made of lead. Each day was more difficult than the one before. Being without Dell was like no pain she had ever felt. It was more intense, more disorienting. She wasn't even doing her job well, the one thing she had always been able to count on in the past. It was as if a part of her had been ripped away.

It's not fair to my friends, either, she reminded herself as she got in her car. Things were picking up here. Belle had even invited Charlie over and let him see the car. Callie was singing, everyone was smiling and an excited hum had begun to thrum through the shop again. Probably because the upcoming Stanson wedding had brought in more business. Once again, Dell had bailed her out. She would have to write a thank-you note. The thought of doing something so formal with Dell made her spirits sink. But she really had to at least pretend to be happy. Her sadness was affecting her friends. That was probably why Callie had sent her on a flower run.

"Nothing like a whole carload of pink roses to cheer a person up," Callie had said, all but pushing her out the door.

Regina had smiled obediently. Now she made her way down the street. It was lunch hour and traffic was heavy. Stalled, Regina looked around her. A billboard high above the street caught her eye. Was that Dell's face?

Her heart began to race, but then she chastised herself. She'd grown used to seeing Dell in her dreams. Now, distraught and lovesick, she was seeing him everywhere. But she shaded her eyes and looked again.

No, it was Dell and in big red letters the sign proclaimed, "Please come home, Regina."

A car honked its horn behind her. She continued down the street. A mobile billboard crossed the intersection in front of her. "Meet me at the mansion," it said.

Someone must be having a joke at her expense. An O'Ryan would never do something as public as this. But as she turned the corner, determined to keep her mind on her task, she got stopped at another street corner. A trio of musicians was singing, nearly blocking traffic. "I'm so sorry if I hurt you, Regina," the man sang. "Please come back and let me tell you how I feel." The sad words and the plaintive melody would be considered sappy and silly by some, but as the singer sang the words, "Come back, Regina," tears began to slide down her face.

A knocking sounded on her window. She looked up to see a police officer outside her car and realized that the light had changed, but when she rolled down the window, the man smiled sympathetically. "He said to tell you that he needs you and that he's sorry if that hurts you. Oh, and he also said to hurry."

Regina blinked and nodded, but she didn't move.

The man tilted his head. "Hurry," he repeated, then nodded toward the line of cars behind her.

"Thank you," she whispered.

The man winked. "Dell's a good guy. Maybe a little crazy today, or maybe a lot crazy, but a good guy. Better hurry before he really gets desperate and calls out the marching band."

Regina swiped at her tears and obediently turned the car. *Dell needed her.*

It wasn't the same as loving her, but...

"I have to see him," she said out loud. She must have messed him up in some way if he was doing something so out of character. At the very least she could explain why she couldn't stay and accept the generous offer of his name. She had wanted to protect her heart, but he deserved to at least know that she wasn't rejecting *him*.

All the way to the mansion, she saw the signs. On billboards, on bicycles, on buses. There was even a blimp.

"Oh, Dell," she whispered. What had she done to him? For the first time ever, she could sympathize with Louella. The man was just too caring for his own good. She should never have allowed him to marry her in the first place. Look what she had driven him to do. Every O'Ryan in history would sit up in their graves and scream at the top of their lungs at the indignity of it all.

With a squeal of tires, Regina pulled the car up in front of the mansion. She ran from the car and threw open the door to the house.

Everything was silent.

"Dell? Dell, are you here?" Her heart was pounding,

racing, practically thumping its way out of her chest. She hadn't seen him in three days but it felt more like three hundred days.

A whimpering sounded.

Regina looked down to see Maynard running toward her. She bent and scooped him up and he began to wag his tail and wriggle and lick at her chin.

"Lucky dog." Dell's deep voice sounded, and Regina whirled to see him leaning casually against a wall at the end of the hall.

"You have a dog," she said, as if her brain had suddenly ceased to function.

He slowly shook his head. "No, you have a dog."

"Oh, yes, your staff doesn't like dogs."

"To hell with my staff. They'll learn to like them. We might end up with two or three or more…if you come back."

Regina closed her eyes. "Dell…"

"I know," he said, his voice harsh. "I know. You can't stay. You told me so."

Her heart was hurting so much. Everything in her soul was hurting. She wanted to stay…so much.

"Just tell me this," he said. "The reason you can't stay, is it because you don't love me?"

He took a step closer, and her mind ceased to function. What was he asking? And how much could she reveal without being irreparably damaged. But wasn't she that already? Shouldn't there be truth among them.

"It was never because I didn't love you," she said, her voice coming out thick and broken.

He took another step closer. "Then is it because you know that I love you and that scares you?"

Her eyes opened wide. "Don't say things that aren't true. You said emotions were too messy."

"They are," he agreed, drawing close enough for her to touch him now. "I've been dying inside since you left. Can't get much messier than that."

"Dell, I—"

"I would never hurt you, Regina."

And then she broke. "Do you think I don't know that? You would never *want* to hurt me, but you couldn't help it. Feeling about you the way I do and knowing that you would just be so darn nice when you didn't feel the same way at all…"

He cleared the small space between them. "How *do* you feel about me?" he demanded.

She stood there, struggling with her pain.

He shook his head. "No, you're right. It's not fair to make you answer that when I all but kidnapped you to get you here. Regina, I love you, heart and soul. I miss you every minute we're apart. I'm not sure if I can live without you, but if being with me hurts you, I—"

His words broke through her pain. She all but flew forward, rose on her toes and kissed him. "That wasn't what was hurting me. It was loving you so much and thinking you could never love me."

Dell's smile was instantaneous and incredulous. He spun her around and planted a hard, demanding kiss on her lips. "I couldn't help loving you. You're everything."

"A friend?" she asked.

"Oh, yes, and a conscience and a lover and the most wonderful gift of a wife a man could ever have."

Regina felt something against her ankle. Maynard was rubbing up against her.

"The dog has taste," Dell said.

"Where did you find him? I know he was already adopted."

He shrugged. "I signed my life away to the friend who had him."

"Oh, Dell, you shouldn't have done that."

"Do you want to give him back?"

"Never. I want to keep him."

"And me?"

"I gave you your chance. Now I'm not letting you go."

Dell's laughter rang out, the most wonderful sound in the world. "That makes me the luckiest man in the world."

Regina smiled and she and Dell came together again, but a rumbling in the street caught their attention. They went to the door and opened it. A crowd had gathered there. A news helicopter was flying overhead. The Belles were at the front of the crowd.

"What's this all about?" someone called.

"Kiss her already," another one called out.

Regina blinked as the cameras snapped and flashed. "Dell, all those signs," she said. "Not an O'Ryan thing to do. It looks as if you got all of Boston's attention."

He wrapped his arm around her waist and pulled her up against him. "I don't care about Boston or the world. Just you. Do I have your attention now?"

"Oh, yes," she said. "Most definitely. Now, did you hear what the man said? It's past time for you to kiss me."

Dell grinned and followed his wife's instructions to the letter, scooping her up against his body as his lips met hers. "I love being married to you," he said when he finally released her.

The crowd went wild. Dell pulled something from his pocket. He bowed to the crowd. He turned to Regina. Obediently she turned and lifted her hair.

"Don't ever leave me again, Regina," he said as he fastened the O'Ryan bride emeralds around her neck and kissed the spot where the clasp rested.

Regina shivered and turned in his arms. "Never again, Dell. Now, can we go inside and begin our marriage again?"

"You have the most wonderful ideas, love," he told her as he closed the door on the cheering crowd and gave Regina his heart forever.

* * * * *

THOROUGHBRED LEGACY
*The stakes are high when it comes to love,
horse racing, family secrets
and broken promises.*

*A new exciting Harlequin continuity series
coming soon!*
Led by New York Times *bestselling author
Elizabeth Bevarly*
FLIRTING WITH TROUBLE

Here's a preview

THE DOOR CLOSED behind them, throwing them into darkness and leaving them utterly alone. And the next thing Daniel knew, he heard himself saying, "Marnie, I'm sorry about the way things turned out in Del Mar."

She said nothing at first, only strode across the room and stared out the window beside him. Although he couldn't see her well in the darkness—he still hadn't switched on a light…but then, neither had she—he imagined her expression was a little preoccupied, a little anxious, a little confused.

Finally, very softly, she said, "Are you?"

He nodded, then, worried she wouldn't be able to see the gesture, added, "Yeah. I am. I should have said goodbye to you."

"Yes, you should have."

Actually, he thought, there were a lot of things he should have done in Del Mar. He'd had *a lot* riding on the Pacific Classic, and even more on his entry, Little Joe, but after meeting Marnie, the Pacific Classic had been the last thing on Daniel's mind. His loss at Del Mar had pretty much ended his career before it had even begun, and he'd had to start all over again, rebuilding from nothing.

He simply had not then and did not now have room in his life for a woman as potent as Marnie Roberts. He was a horseman first and foremost. From the time he was a schoolboy, he'd known what he wanted to do with his life—be the best possible trainer he could be.

He had to make sure Marnie understood—and he understood, too—why things had ended the way they had eight years ago. He just wished he could find the words to do that. Hell, he wished he could find the *thoughts* to do that.

"You made me forget things, Marnie, things that I really needed to remember. And that scared the hell out of me. Little Joe should have won the Classic. He was by far the best horse entered in that race. But I didn't give him the attention he needed and deserved that week, because all I could think about was you. Hell, when I woke up that morning all I wanted to do was lie there and look at you, and then wake you up and make love to you again. If I hadn't left when I did—the way I did—I might still be lying there in that bed with you, thinking about nothing else."

"And would that be so terrible?" she asked.

"Of course not," he told her. "But that wasn't why I was in Del Mar," he repeated. "I was in Del Mar to win a race. That was my job. And my work was the most important thing to me."

She said nothing for a moment, only studied his face in the darkness as if looking for the answer to a very important question. Finally she asked, "And what's the most important thing to you now, Daniel?"

Wasn't the answer to that obvious? "My work," he answered automatically.

She nodded slowly. "Of course," she said softly. "That is, after all, what you do best."

Her comment, too, puzzled him. She made it sound as if being good at what he did was a bad thing.

She bit her lip thoughtfully, her eyes fixed on his, glimmering in the scant moonlight that was filtering through the window. And damned if Daniel didn't find himself wanting to pull her into his arms and kiss her. But as much as it might have felt as if no time had passed since Del Mar, there were eight years between now and then. And eight years was a long time in the best of circumstances. For Daniel and Marnie, it was virtually a lifetime.

So Daniel turned and started for the door, then halted. He couldn't just walk away and leave things as they were, unsettled. He'd done that eight years ago and regretted it.

"It *was* good to see you again, Marnie," he said softly. And since he was being honest, he added, "I hope we see each other again."

She didn't say anything in response, only stood silhouetted against the window with her arms wrapped around her in a way that made him wonder whether she was doing it because she was cold, or if she just needed something—someone—to hold on to. In either case, Daniel understood. There was an emptiness clinging to him that he suspected would be there for a long time.

* * * * *

THOROUGHBRED LEGACY
coming soon wherever books are sold!

Thoroughbred *Legacy*

Launching in June 2008

A dramatic new 12-book continuity that embodies the American Dream.

Meet the Prestons, owners of Quest Stables, a successful horse-racing and breeding empire. But the lives, loves and reputations of this hardworking family are put at risk when a breeding scandal unfolds.

Flirting with Trouble

by *New York Times* bestselling author

ELIZABETH BEVARLY

Eight years ago, publicist Marnie Roberts spent seven days of bliss with Australian horse trainer Daniel Whittleson. But just as quickly, he disappeared. Now Marnie is heading to Australia to finally confront the man she's never been able to forget.

The stakes are high when it comes to love, horse racing, family secrets and broken promises.

A new exciting Harlequin continuity series coming soon!

www.eHarlequin.com

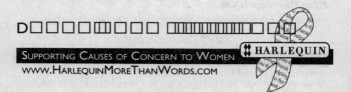

HARLEQUIN
More Than Words

"Autism—a national
health crisis.
Get informed.
Get involved. I am."

—**Curtiss Ann Matlock,** author

Curtiss Ann wrote "A Place in This World," inspired by Dr. Ricki Robinson.
*Through her practice and her work with **Autism Speaks,** Dr. Ricki has*
provided hope to countless parents and children coping with autism.

Look for "*A Place in This World*" in
More Than Words, Vol. 4,
available in April 2008 at eHarlequin.com
or wherever books are sold.

SUPPORTING CAUSES OF CONCERN TO WOMEN   **HARLEQUIN**
WWW.HARLEQUINMORETHANWORDS.COM

MTW07ROB2

REQUEST YOUR FREE BOOKS!
2 FREE NOVELS PLUS 2
FREE GIFTS!

HARLEQUIN ROMANCE®

From the Heart, For the Heart

YES! Please send me 2 FREE Harlequin Romance® novels and my 2 FREE gifts (gifts are worth about $10). After receiving them, if I don't wish to receive any more books, I can return the shipping statement marked "cancel". If I don't cancel, I will receive 4 brand-new novels every month and be billed just $3.32 per book in the U.S. or $3.80 per book in Canada, plus 25¢ shipping and handling per book and applicable taxes, if any*. That's a savings of over 15% off the cover price! I understand that accepting the 2 free books and gifts places me under no obligation to buy anything. I can always return a shipment and cancel at any time. Even if I never buy another book, the two free books and gifts are mine to keep forever.

114 HDN ERQW   314 HDN ERQ9

Name	(PLEASE PRINT)	
Address		Apt. #
City	State/Prov.	Zip/Postal Code

Signature (if under 18, a parent or guardian must sign)

Mail to the **Harlequin Reader Service:**
IN U.S.A.: P.O. Box 1867, Buffalo, NY 14240-1867
IN CANADA: P.O. Box 609, Fort Erie, Ontario L2A 5X3

Not valid to current subscribers of Harlequin Romance books.

Want to try two free books from another line?
Call 1-800-873-8635 or visit www.morefreebooks.com.

* Terms and prices subject to change without notice. N.Y. residents add applicable sales tax. Canadian residents will be charged applicable provincial taxes and GST. This offer is limited to one order per household. All orders subject to approval. Credit or debit balances in a customer's account(s) may be offset by any other outstanding balance owed by or to the customer. Please allow 4 to 6 weeks for delivery. Offer available while quantities last.

Your Privacy: Harlequin Books is committed to protecting your privacy. Our Privacy Policy is available online at www.eHarlequin.com or upon request from the Reader Service. From time to time we make our lists of customers available to reputable third parties who may have a product or service of interest to you. If you would prefer we not share your name and address, please check here. ☐

HR08

HARLEQUIN *Presents*

Don't forget Harlequin Presents EXTRA
now brings you a powerful new collection
every month featuring four books!

Be sure not to miss any of the titles in

In the Greek Tycoon's Bed,
available May 13:

THE GREEK'S FORBIDDEN BRIDE
by Cathy Williams

THE GREEK TYCOON'S UNEXPECTED WIFE
by Annie West

THE GREEK TYCOON'S VIRGIN MISTRESS
by Chantelle Shaw

THE GIANNAKIS BRIDE
by Catherine Spencer

HARLEQUIN *Romance*

Coming Next Month

**Enjoy a gondola ride along the canals of Venice,
join a royal wedding party or take a romantic stroll through the
streets of London…all next month with Harlequin Romance®!**

#4027 THE PREGNANCY PROMISE by Barbara McMahon
Unexpectedly Expecting!

What's on *your* wish list for the perfect guy? At the top of Lianne's is that
he will be a great father…to the child she longs for. In the first of this
heartwarming duet, Lianne's deepest desire may be fulfilled from the most
unexpected of places…by her gorgeous boss, Tray!

#4028 THE ITALIAN'S CINDERELLA BRIDE by Lucy Gordon
Heart to Heart

A flash of lightning brings a young woman to Count Pietro Bagnelli's *palazzo*.
Though Pietro's turned against the world, he can't reject this bedraggled waif.
But can Ruth find a fairy-tale ending with the proud, damaged count?

#4029 SOS MARRY ME! by Melissa McClone
The Wedding Planners

Only Mr. Right will do for wedding-dress designer Serena, and free-spirited
pilot Kane meets none of her criteria. Then he is forced to perform a crash
landing! Stranded with Serena, there's no denying the chemistry!

#4030 HER ROYAL WEDDING WISH by Cara Colter
By Royal Appointment

Princess Shoshauna craves the freedom to marry for love, not duty. Then,
suddenly in danger, she is whisked to safety by unsuitable but daring soldier
Jake Ronan. She may owe him her life, but will she give him her hand…
in marriage?

#4031 SAYING YES TO THE MILLIONAIRE by Fiona Harper
A Bride for All Seasons

Challenged by a friend, cautious Fern ends up on a four-day treasure hunt
with dreamy Josh Adams! Daredevil Josh never stays in one place—or with
one woman—for long. Could Fern be the exception to the rule?

#4032 HER BABY, HIS PROPOSAL by Teresa Carpenter
Baby on Board

Navy SEAL Brock Sullivan's code of honor leads him to gallantly propose
to pregnant stranger Jesse, who needs his help and protection. But what
begins as a marriage of convenience starts to grow very complicated when
Brock comes home injured, needing loving care….

HRCNM0508